Praise for Luisa V~l
and *He Wh*

"Luisa Valenzuela is the heiress of ....ican fiction. She wears an opulent, baroque crown, but her feet are naked."
—Carlos Fuentes

"Luisa Valenzuela explores the terrain where love and violence, erotic pleasure and death, exist perilously close to each other. . . . Valenzuela plays with words, turns them inside out, weaves them into sensuous webs."
—*Voice Literary Supplement*

"*He Who Searches* is as stunning a portrait of Latin America and its strange, magical realities as the portraits found in Gabriel García Márquez's *One Hundred Years of Solitude* and Carlos Fuentes' *Terra Nostra*. And like those novels, it is also a work of universal appeal."
—*San Francisco Chronicle*

"This novel . . . is a prime example of contemporary Latin American fiction. Its major themes are love, identity, reality, time, existence, and death, expressed with an innovative narrative structure and point of view, through myriad symbols and against a political and feminist backdrop."
—*Choice*

"To read her is to enter *our* reality fully, where plurality surpasses the limitations of the past; to read her is to participate in a search for Latin American identity, which offers its rewards beforehand. Luisa Valenzuela's books are our present, but they also contain much of our future; there is true resplendence, true love, true freedom on each of her pages."
—Julio Cortázar

Luisa Valenzuela

He Who Searches

Translated by Helen R. Lane

Dalkey Archive Press

Originally published as *Como en la guerra* (Buenos Aires, 1977). © 1977 by Luisa Valenzuela.

English translation by Helen R. Lane originally published as part of *Strange Things Happen Here* (Harcourt Brace Jovanovich, 1979). English translation © 1979 by Harcourt Brace Jovanovich. Reprinted by permission of the publishers.

First Dalkey Archive edition, 1987
        second printing, 1988
        third printing, 1990
        fourth printing, 1994

ISBN 0-916583-20-1
LC 86-073237

NATIONAL
ENDOWMENT
FOR THE
ARTS

Partially funded by grants from the Illinois Arts Council and the National Endowment for the Arts.

Dalkey Archive Press
Campus Box 4241
Normal, IL 61790-4241

Printed on permanent/durable acid-free paper and bound in the United States of America.

Page zero

"I wasn't there. I don't know anything, I swear I had nothing to do with her."

"You were seen entering her house late at night. In Barcelona. Twice a week for several months. What were you looking for? Talk!"

"What I know about her can't be of any interest to you."

"Shut up, you fag priest, you fruit, you little egghead. Don't waste our time. Talk."

an enormous hand approaches his face, about to explode. No, not in a blow but in a caress on his forehead. When he was little, not today, no.

Nature doesn't have any giant closeups, so the individual has to choose the perspective that best suits his mood. The individual looks for the big closeup (infinite isolation); he can use mechanical devices or focus his eyes carefully.

A giant hand is therefore something that belongs to us all, it is usually sought after and cared for. A closeup is a step forward, the instant prior to coming to grips with things, the insurmountable barrier. Suddenly the hand that is approaching dissolves and we are inside it, we enter a universe formed by its life-line, its heart-line, fate, and a badly drawn furrow that represents the brain. The hand is the vehicle and it is not easy to be transported by it to the bottom of things and enter a diffuse world where I reshape and recompose myself.

. . .

There have been better times, I must admit, lucid moments when my duty did not consist of banishing pain—quite the contrary—and they were times spent with her. "I don't know a thing!" I shout to them to prove that I exist because they have forgotten me and are concentrating on the soles of my feet or on my testicles.

Raped by a gun barrel. This sad fate appears to be mine and I scream with pain, never out of fear. They want to get at me through panic; to escape this trap I concentrate on the life throbbing above my eyebrows and let them have the rest of my body. My body is dead below the eyebrows, dead long before that man twists the revolver in my guts and laughs as he says I'm going to pull the trigger now. IMGOINGTOPULLTHETRIGGER-NOW echoes everywhere surrounds me it's become an acoustic chamber triggernow triggernow the walls send back to me and I'll get even with the walls I'll explode on them and spatter shit all over them. What a great consolation. What a marvelous splattering when he pulls the triggernow triggernow triggernow

I. The Discovery

She was born the way we're all born, complaining against her/our bitch of a fate. There was no way of establishing whether each wail was a complaint at having entered the world or at something more subtle, like anguish for the human race—her brothers—on entering this other far more collective amniotic liquid called air. It's not known whether he/she had to be grabbed by the feet and shaken so as to release the cry. But there's not the slightest shadow of a doubt that the cry came, because this cry continues to resound and threatens to cover up the absurd wells of silence that can be heard in these parts. What portion of the globe saw her birth? In her dreams palpable and other coordinates exist, not always interfering with each other: the ones in her dreams have runaway horses; in the palpable ones were an ice-van that left a puddle of water outside the door, a house around the corner from some minor mysteries, and the shoemaker's shop where she took refuge on running away from home when she was five. An abortive escape but since then flight seems to be her fate and until she was twelve she went around tripping up death. Then death left her, abandoned her—the same little girl who had cleverly lain in ambush for it and trimmed its cat-mustache—made as she was to torment cats until the day a black cat almost tore out one of her eyes—a black cat—with one swipe of its paw.

As for spiders, that's a separate chapter or perhaps part of a chapter to come since spiders also have their say in this story (the story of a life, not much of anything).

. . .

When she was small they opened her head to see what was inside and presumably found nothing because they let her go with a hole behind one ear unconcerned that her soul might escape through it, or an idea or whatever the hell there may be inside a (human?) head. Conclusion: they had found nothing escapable in there and they left the trepanation unattended. So for many years she had to confront the waves with rubber stoppers in her ears to keep the water out (it may be bad to have an empty head, but it's worse to have one full of liquid). A hollow head has its advantages, sometimes it's a martyrdom and sometimes it hammers like crazy the way hers did, making her believe that her neighbor the shoemaker was working at night when the hammer was her own blood, pounding away. Blood she did have, nor did she lose much with the passage of time although she managed to gamble it away—or so she thinks—for nobly unnecessary causes.

To return to her head, we now transcribe a few of her notes that may be of use to some scholar pondering these lines. The text reads as follows:

there are heads for everyone, one per person when nothing is done *manu militari* and they are expropriated from them by licit means: the executioner's ax, the guillotine, and other inventions of man for man's sake. But leaving aside the cranial cavity, we must never forget the sacrosanct duty of the sacrum and the iliac: to wriggle in a ball without heads or tails and to no end.

with whom shall I be in love today, with whom tomorrow? why am I tiring this arm that isn't mine and pretending not to have noticed those remote regions where the sun never sets or drinks orange juice? a sun without orange juice, heaven help us, where is its color, its vitality?

if someday I manage to read my handwriting, to decipher my message, then I'll know obscure secrets that I want to transmit to myself. in the month of August, in the antipodes, I can know nothing of those who in sublime moments like this one bet their boots (their brains) in some precise, untimely game. the seven athletes are there, dressed in blue, in their best clothes, forming a human tower in slow movements like automatons and that is precisely what they are, there is the giant wheel that turns round and round, the lights of the little train on the night of epiphany, like the tango, like human wretchedness, injectable poverty. I have found the drugs that society consumes: intravenous misery, cries by way of the mouth, caustic suppositories. in the war of ideas it's never the most intelligent who wins but rather the sharpest, the irredentist, the monkeyman who climbs among the branches and so keeps his distance from every predetermined sensation. the a priori fanciers of sleepless nights, and night is waiting for me at distant street corners, it accompanies me in my acts of exile such as sniffing dogs' behinds.

I learned this healthy habit from them. I have no reason to feel proud or ashamed. to feel neither proud nor ashamed is the perfect state of equilibrium on the tightrope of life. one ball behind and another in front, as a counterweight. one step more and I'll fall, one less and I know where they'll have to look for me, those few who devote themselves to the study of other people's habits (one's own habits are harder to confess, protected like a tube of thick, ductile paste). but I no longer dance to that tune, and I take comfort in the invisible things of this world; I do so to calm my inner wrath, the horror that is given off by my obscure forms. they are all on the ground, sitting in a semicircle, waiting for the moon to come out to celebrate it in chorus. they are gray, blurred, they would have nothing to do with the dance that moves the tops of the pines—the smell of pines, their ancestral perfume. I wonder what the tops of the singing trees suggest to them—a garden of still water? A prayer wheel? I for my part would like something slow that would slip through my fingers and stretch all through the night its need to be, its immemorial midday quiet.

Her texts almost never coincide with the dates to which we refer, but they are pertinent, no matter how impertinent they may seem. We have our own methods of analysis and we ask you to kindly respect them, as we ask that you respect the unconscious work of our patient.

. . .

We have gathered few memories of her childhood. She experienced first conscious pleasure at the age of two when after much reflection she opened the refrigerator door, took out eggs and dropped them on the floor one by one; broken at her feet, the eggs gave her profound enjoyment. There's no point in interpreting this transparent fact, since she herself notes that the pleasure in breaking eggs has been repeated in a metaphorical way at different times in her life.

Lemon flower, living blood. From her earliest childhood we have been able to gather little information to place under our microscope. This is an incomplete sample that gives us an imprecise idea of the illness that must have been manifest at that time.

"Is it because they told me that they carry their houses on their backs and leave a wake of silvery spittle to make the path behind them that I love them? No one understands me or them and that's why I love them and want to take them everywhere with me. They are inside their houses inside themselves, they lay transparent eggs, they are transparent when they are born with the two little horns like antennae and they crawl across my hand, up my arm. I see them now, I remember all this for you, doctor."

"Don't call me doctor, call me Pepe."

(We must hurry the transference along, we said to ourselves impatiently. The sick woman can't be left a prey to her affects.)

So I was obliged, if you'll permit me personal references, to devote myself to psychoanalysis in a secret way, for her sake. Not that my studies didn't let me do so. They allow me that and much more, such as following my investigation through all the twists and turns of the psyche and a few extra as well that we'll discover in due course.

That's why I used to arrive at her room in the Pasaje des Escudellers late at night; those were hard times for both of us, except that she could know nothing of me and I wanted to know everything about her. She had to vent her feelings with someone after long hours of listening to other people's stories in the cabaret across the way. She earned little as a waitress, so I didn't charge her anything, which kept it from being as orthodox as it might have been, but also kept it from being rigidly dogmatic. Bear in mind that other details provided additional flexibility to the analysis and allowed me to advance rapidly, namely:

(a) She didn't know that I was giving her therapy.
(b) She didn't know who I was.
(c) She didn't know that I was one and the same person every time I saw her, because I appeared—in the wee hours of Monday and Thursday mornings—in different disguises.

The choice of disguises was based strictly on chance, unlike the choice of hours, which was established after a lengthy prior investigation: we hid in a doorway watching her go in and out, we scrupulously noted down her every movement, her dress, her life behind the red curtains of her house or in the dim light of the bar with cocktail waitresses. And so we were able to determine the best hour to find her at home, when she'd be exhausted and for that reason more inclined to reveal her unconscious mechanisms. Three A.M. seemed to be the ideal hour, on Monday and Thursday (and occasionally on Saturdays).

It's essential that you understand the sacrifice this labor required of us. The author of this study, a humble professor of semiotics who's at your service, couldn't let his wife in on his new investigation, so he had to steal through the night like a criminal and go down the darkest streets alone while his wife snored peacefully in their double bed. (Her bed was a modest studio couch, though it knew as much of life and love, or more, than any of the spacious beds boasted of around here.) And our wife, I repeat, lay snoring in our bed (later she says she's a light sleeper and the slightest noise wakes her up), and there we were sneaking out of the house in different disguises because she wouldn't have accepted us otherwise.

Everything began (but can these things ever begin at any one time, can the one reason for our existence have a beginning?), apparently everything began after a long period of teaching in London, when we were giving a boring, censored course in Barcelona. Something altogether routine, our only consolation being to sneak out of the house on certain nights—this was before the incident that foreshadows my approaching her—to have a few drinks in the Barrio Chino. That night we didn't want to have anything to drink, we preferred to sit in the Plaza Real and watch the couples (our interest was scientific, naturally). Suddenly we saw her, suddenly I saw her and leaped back fifteen years to my beloved Buenos Aires, a leap that left me clinging to a dark, profound look, a hole-look into which I fell like a scatterbrain (understand that I was fifteen years younger, and that one must get to know the master and pardon certain of his defects if one is to learn all he has to teach). That was the beginning of our meeting—I looked at her, I approached her and took her by the arm, I felt her altogether mine, and asked her: Do we know each other? and she answered, intimidated: I don't believe so. I confused you with someone else. And I, a bully at that time, said: I didn't ask you if we knew each other from before, but proposed instead that we get to know each other now.

We got to know each other all right. But only in a relative way because she lapsed into silence when we were together and then I began losing sight of her and lost her altogether and it mattered little to me

(it mattered little to me? Rereading this confession I realize what I'm saying and I musn't permit myself lies—especially now, when I'm trying to get the truth out of her).

. . .

This may explain the emotion of a man like me, usually so calm and collected, when right square in the middle of the Plaza Real, in Barcelona, the same eyes appeared before me, the same sort of look in her eye. And so you must excuse my trembling as I approached her and asked her Do we know each other? in the hope of awakening old memories. But she answered If you think so, beautiful, I'll make you a nice price, and I turned halfway around and ran and almost burst into tears because what else could I do? I didn't want to get the splinters of a broken dream hurled smack in my face, but the next night I followed her at a distance and for months studied her conduct which seemed normal considering the seriousness of the case.

So we were able to begin this scientific report by speaking of her birth, as is only proper. In our second encounter we had every weapon within grasp—the indispensable interest, the free-floating attention—to wangle out of her all the information essential for the study of her character and conduct, with a view to effective therapeutic action. Naturally we needed additional information regarding her early childhood and her fantasies, in order to ascertain whether what drove her to the life she was leading and what forced her to write compulsively (graphomania) had one and the same cause or were one and the same effect.

One night—perhaps the eighth when, so to speak, I'd come running at her beck and call—we didn't have the heart or strength to disguise ourselves. Disguising oneself in a different way each Monday and Thursday and occasionally on Saturday wears one out. At any rate, we left the house dressed as usual: blue suit, tie, brief case. Except that in the brief case was a well-wrapped bottle of wine.

I stroll up and down the Calle des Escudellers waiting for the clock to strike three before entering the Pasaje. She must not be home yet. I walk around, realizing the street's a mess and that

I like it. The women whistle as I go by and a while ago a hand reached out from a dark doorway and touched my ass and it wasn't exactly a dainty feminine hand; there's a smell of fried food and the noise is unbearable. In her room it's as if noise were forbidden and not much air can get in either so as not to break the isolation. When three o'clock finally strikes on a distant bell tower, we enter the narrow little side street, go up the stairs two by two, stride down the long hallway and then, our strength nearly exhausted and with a sinking heart, ring a doorbell and apologize for disturbing her. A surprise! She has on a bright red wig, she who never smokes has a long cigarette holder in her hand and a green velvet dress clinging to her ample hips. She's fooled more by my everyday outfit than by any of the previous ones, she immediately invests it with mythical attributes and completely frustrates my attempt to get closer to her, to offer myself naked—I mean with my usual clothes on—as I pretend to be or at least believe I am or believe I pretend I am. She doesn't allow me this over-confidence; for some obscure motive that we'll try to get to the bottom of later, she seems able to communicate only with archetypal beings. On seeing me she immediately offers me the possibility of a new mask, or rather she forces me to accept it: "The insurance agent! Come in, come in, I can't pay you today but I can offer you a chair. You must be tired out, working till all hours of the night, do come in."

In her clothes, her face, the objects in the room I see that she longs to be an old fashioned cocotte, and I try to go on with her game. Green looks well on her, the wig matches the embroidered bedspread which she surely brought with her from Argentina. She hasn't yet mentioned a city, much less a country, even though everything around her cries out Argentina, Argentina, and no matter what guise she assumes, or what accent, I smell it immediately.

(what's the matter with this country that makes us all flee from it and burns us inside? What makes us wander about the world, tramps of love, without even wanting to recognize

each other, denying ourselves to each other? What does it mean
to be . . . ?)

Let's see if you'll leave me in peace to write my story!

Now I'm the insurance collector. What sort of insurance can
this madwoman have, against what can she be trying to protect
herself, what catastrophes does she think lie in wait for her?
Insurance against fire? Against loneliness? Insurance against
theft, tonsillitis, syphilis? Insurance against unbearable pains of
the soul? All right, then, I'm collecting for insurance that isn't
paid for in money, but in much more valuable currency such as
gratitude or total surrender. She must have no secrets from me,
that's my price; we'll see what I can find out about her once
she lays aside all traces of her prudishness, her inner censorship,
and above all self-denial. I'm a god to her, and she knows it now
and metaphorically kisses the soles of my feet—she offers to take
off my shoes. Make yourself comfortable, she says, this chair's
the best—the only chair in the room—and I say to her, as if it
had just popped into my head: one of my clients gave me a
bottle of wine, if you'd like to share it with me . . .

On nights when she acts like an old fashioned cocotte, red wine
is the best recipe. She gets out a can of pâté and we begin our
modest orgy, our endless chatter.

It takes only two glasses, we've proved that, to open the flood-
gates and let the ideas and sensations flow, without her knowing
that they'll be analyzed by us later. On finishing the second
glass, she asked if it wouldn't be more comfortable for us—for
her and me, that is—if she sat on our—my—knee. We must
have answered in the affirmative, or at least not have refused
with sufficient firmness, for it was after being on our—my—knee
for a time and then leaping up as if to see what was hidden in
my trousers, that she told *the story of papa's friend.* I tried to
accept this story, which I transcribe in the appendix, as a simple
confidence without making any interpretation. This displeased

15

her and she confessed that it hadn't happened to her but to her girlfriend. I then tried to get her to associate, because what was the point of foisting off somebody else's story? I said to her:

(1) You are investing me with the characteristics of the mythical father.

(2) One must always take the phallus into account as the signifier *par excellence*. Or as Jacques Lacan says, "the signifier destined to designate the overall effects of the signified."

(3) You are attempting to take refuge in the life-traumas of another person because your neurosis doesn't allow you to face up to your own contingencies.

That night, after we learned that *the story of papa's friend* hadn't really happened to her, we insisted that she try to see more clearly this characteristic need of hers to share other people's lives.

"I like to put myself inside people to learn what they think," she said.

"To put yourself inside *me* to learn what *I* think, you mean."

"Yes, and inside you I find fear, tenderness, a shell."

"As Dr. Salomon Resnik says, putting oneself inside another is what gives us the so-called telepathic powers."

We noted that as with many another learned quotation, our store of knowledge didn't surprise her in the least, coming as it did from an ordinary albeit nocturnal insurance collector.

Those Monday and Thursday night tasks proved arduous, particularly if one takes into account the need to vary the disguises and continually use our imagination. Therefore on a certain Thursday when we had run out of disguises and were forced to leave the house in a hurry, we grabbed a fancy dressing gown of our spouse (Beatriz) and one of her winter nightcaps. Luckily we didn't have to walk the streets that way—what an embarrassment that would have been! We were able to put on the peignoir and the cap on the dark landing in front of her door. But a couple of girls passing by—some poor sluts—shouted something that I refused to grasp, thank heaven. Did I say refused to? On occasion, we too make slips of the tongue.

She opened the door and appeared in some strange way to recognize us. She stroked the salmon-colored velvet peignoir, and stood there looking at us making certain projections, perhaps. Naturally we didn't want her to stroke us too much: for our own sake and for the sake of the noble mission that had brought us to her. Then with gentle words we poked about in her fantasies, tried to take her back to childhood and certain pleasures, employing laughter and flattery and the wheedling tone of an elderly homosexual. We spoke of meals, not forgetting to mention gluttony which seemed important to her and she confessed, not without embarrassment, that her favorite meals at the age of three were mussels and hot dogs. Perhaps she herself will discover the symbolic relationships that are so glaringly evident; perhaps she will intuit how much the primal scene has to do with this memory, the hot dogs being the father and the mussels the mother. Even so we didn't want to press the point too far, so we let her go on remembering, going back in her childhood to the time when she pushed a swinging door for the first time and was amazed at her power. Then we did in fact intervene, in a sly way, and asked her to begin to associate:

. . .

"Sometimes they isolate, sometimes they join together. If I were a door, if I knew I'd be taken by the hinges, could I open and close myself with the expression of a sad oyster? I ask you this because doors are also a question, unknown quantities that reveal themselves when one opens them and goes through them or else they don't reveal anything and that's better: not walking into the truth because the truth is demanding, the truth drags the worst out of us—the only thing that belongs to us. I am outside the truth, outside of time, but that's no reason to make a face or not to smile at people who pass by: I want to give all of them everything I have even if that displeases them, even if others criticize me. Except that others should be less selfish and shatter their inner armor, turn into mollusks without shells, real defenseless beings."

How it pleases us when she comes up with such highly elaborate things. Then she calms down, offers us another glass of wine, another cup of coffee without waiting for an answer.

ing intensely at fashioning her legend,

not take a little walk? I need air, lots

ind much air, my dear, in these narrow,

w how to find air. Lots of air."

it. I'd rather stay here. Or go home, but

it."

hairpins—black hair that night—threw
ders, and left with a stubborn, friendless
she murmured something like *there are
and don't know it and claim afterward*
but we aren't c

I stood at the window and saw her walking away (she knew
how to move her hips), cross the street, look in all directions,
and then something distracted me and I lost sight of her. I
stretched out on the bed and closed my eyes to rest (one mustn't
forget that very likely she had sweet little dreams during the day
while I had to work, and this nocturnal investigation threatened
to drain my strength). But the scientific spirit won out over
fatigue and before long we began searching the room for signs
that might make our job go faster. We spent little time studying
the décor even though we'd never allowed ourselves to observe
it before lest our curiosity leap into her awareness like a dark
spider and put her on her guard.

The night protected us: with our ears pricked we'd hear the
footsteps coming up the stairs. And having taken infinite precautions, we opened one drawer and then another. Amid pairs
of stockings and panties we found notebooks, a great many notebooks, of all colors and sizes, filled with uneven handwriting.
The hand at times grew inordinately large and then got smaller

19

and smaller until it turned into insect tracks. A graphologist would have said "unstable cyclothymic behavior, a tendency to night terrors." Would he have detected schizophrenia behind all this? Graphologists don't interest us—there are more hermetic sciences with less chance of disagreement.

(But we wish at this point to make clear that all the written material presented in this report has been furnished by the patient herself. It has never been obtained behind her back or against her will.) Therefore our search on Thursday night served only to further inform us, to open up a broader panorama, not to transgress the limits that we had fixed out of ethical scruples. Scham, the demon of modesty, used to overcome us back in those days, so we were petrified when we suddenly saw her facing us, not having made a sound, not even when she opened the door behind the red curtain. She caught us *in flagrante:* we were holding one of her carved hands in our hand, staring at it as if trying to extract a secret from it.

"Are you interested in hands, too?" she asked as if nothing had happened. "I think they're closely connected with the cosmos. I have symbols of hands from every religion, from all over the world. If you like, I'll show you my collection."

The carved hands were forgotten then, and also her collection, another of her favorite subjects that we promise to return to in a moment. But what happened that night was too much for our feeble understanding. She opened her shopping bag and took out a bottle of ordinary Argentine wine and some tamales wrapped in corn husks (in Barcelona! who ever saw such a thing!). Her smile as she put these treasures on the table was so special, so out of the ordinary. Did we dare ask where they had come from, where she had been able to get such things? No, we didn't. I stood there staring at her and then she said, guessing my thoughts: "You refused to come with me, so don't ask silly questions now. There are people like me who know how to travel: we're in the minority; the majority don't even know how to get to the corner without actually going there. All so trivial. So flat.

If only they knew that one always gets what one wants but never when one wants it. It's enough to do as I do and want things at the wrong time. I think I wrote something about that but I don't remember. I write and forget, so I'm amazed when I read my texts again, and I don't always have the heart to. What's the matter with a writer? Can he at times give the analyst the noblest material, the perishable material that can open the doors to other memories? Is the writer Sesame? He is words then, the open sesame behind which we find ourselves at the mercy of others for the happiness of all. There's no point in believing in omnipotence or in magic faculties and all that junk: one need only allow oneself to be carried away by the current, to be dissolved in the Other."

Now we had time enough only to return to the tamales and Argentine wine and gulp them down, without taking into account their unexpected source.

As I left her house I made the following notes:

—For the first time she has spoken of her writings and described herself, or at least questioned herself, as a writer.
—She appears to have parapsychological powers for which she has an Olympian disdain.
—For the first time she has spoken of psychoanalysis, perhaps unconsciously recognizing my mission though she denies it on a conscious level.
—Why do I resort to every imaginable subterfuge to help her in her denial?
—She offers to show me certain things (the collection of hands). Will she ever allow me to read what she writes?
—Will I be able to replace my pocket tape recorder, which has so many flaws, with a better, more obvious one? This would mean admitting that I record all our conversations, which may inhibit her. But doesn't she know already? I suspect that she suspects, because at times she speaks in too highflown a manner, as if saying things meant to endure.

And what part do *I* play in all this? What instrument? What flute, what trombone in an orchestra of cats meowing at the moon, cats in heat, not allowing ourselves the slightest jealousy, neither she nor I, in the opposed positions in which we find ourselves?

Those nights, for me, had a totally different color from all other nights. At times I walked about without thinking what day of the week it was and then suddenly a reddish glow at the far end of a street, lights more yellow than yellow, would remind me that Monday was beginning, or Thursday, and I had a mission to fulfill no matter how gratuitous it might seem. I wonder if she felt something similar, if on leaving the cabaret after work she knew when it was time to wait for me, when I was going to arrive in one way or another, in some form or other, not necessarily the same from her point of view but even so always expected. I observed that on some nights she went off with men from the bar, that on others she collapsed in bed dead tired without taking her shoes off. I wonder then why I always found her fresh, in an atmosphere thick with incense perhaps prepared especially for me. Could she be waiting for me? Could she be thinking of me when I was far away? Can she know that we are one, multiplied only for her sake?

tonight is a night for murder. the heat is just right, like an oven ready for a body to be thrust in—not to take the skin off or slip the body into it, but to shove it all the way inside and wait for it to burn. I'll be a good widow (unlike other widows), I'll burn another in my place to celebrate my life. it would be nice to kill him with one blow but that's impossible; it would be nice to mix poisons and compound the ultimate lethal potion but that's impossible. I can't get hold of poisons and I run the risk of making him sick and vomiting and it may have a delayed effect and I'll miss his sublime agony. letting him go off to die in his own house, in his own bed—think of that! I'll have to use a pistol, if I put it to his temple when he's not looking and act quickly he won't have time to think. I'll polish the pistol, I'll load it and wait for the moment, the moment? I should persuade him to come Tuesday at midnight, the neighborhood festival and the fireworks will muffle the sound of the shot. his death will be just another splash of fireworks, another game, and I can keep his body in the closet for a few days, I can do with him as I please though I still don't know what. I can study him, find out what he's up to, what he's like inside, what he wants. at last a man for me alone, at last a dream come true.

and then I'll leave this city, this country, as I've done so many times before, and when somebody comes in here because the rent is overdue or because the smell is terrible, not only will I have gotten away but they won't even know who I am, who I've been, let alone who I'm about to be. he'll be a bridge for me, a good reason to go away because I'm settling down too much, I'm clinging to the old shell, to the Gothic Quarter, to everything that has nothing to do with the times we live in. and what about him? I can only say that he'll be the ideal sacrificial victim. I didn't look for him, he came of his own free will to put himself in these wolf's jaws of mine, and moreover I'm sure that nobody knows about these nightly visits of his. I hand over to him little pieces of my own life and of some of those I assume when the night is hot and humid and I don't feel like being a person. I see him arriving in different disguises and pretend not to recognize him, but none of those who see him at my door will take him to be himself (he hides among the shadows, comes secretly, this is the sort of adventure that one never confesses to). even I don't know who he is and I'm careful not to ask. sometimes he's the postman bringing a telegram with the wrong name, the gas meter man, a cheap transvestite or an elegant one, or a fireman lost amid flames that have been put out; he's those who exist at three in the morning, as if I didn't know. every time he goes away he's left behind part of his outfit: a hat one time, the cape another, the cosmetic kit, that ridiculous feather boa he wore the second time he came in drag. I could never give him back his belongings because I don't want to destroy his eagerness to be different every time.

Because of the aforesaid, and because my fingernails are long now and he's asking for it, I think his time has come. He should begin to tremble: I'm going to shoot off my whole being as I squeeze the trigger.

Doesn't anybody in this building have any prejudices? Doesn't anybody ever shout? What silence, what horrible silence on the stairs that twist and turn, and along the endless corridors that lead to her door. There are ninety-four steps, I count them every time, but the landings are far apart, you have to go down narrow halls, open doors, and turn to the left and right to get to her room under the gables. And up there she waits for me fresh as a flower, smiling, as if she hadn't had to run upstairs a few minutes before. Many times I arrive right on her heels and find her cool and collected, her clothes changed, a wig in place, her face made up, and lights on that make her look like a bird or a wolf.

Today the wolf face is more wolfish than ever and her curly hair straight and disheveled, longer than ever, and not fake. I'm myself, today I'm tired of making myself plural, of playing therapist. I have on a pair of old trousers and an unbuttoned shirt. I ring the soft bell—almost inaudible—her doorbell; as usual she slowly opens the bronze peephole and contemplates me as if a man at her door was unheard of. After opening the door she continues to stare at me, and I feel that the fifty minutes that I set aside for her will be spent that way, the two of us staring at each other in a wave of hatred that glows from her eyes. Suddenly I spy red spots on her hands and think of blood. I'm not alarmed; I'm proud of never being alarmed at the whims of a patient. I know that tonight I'm not the one to begin the dialogue. She looks at me, takes out a pair of red gloves from a box, and puts them on. She keeps on looking at me, carefully smoothing the gloves over her fingers, stroking one hand with the other. I note that the armchair I always sit in—the only one, the chair in which I'm sitting—has been moved out of its usual corner and is now in the middle of the room. She walks around me in circles as she finishes putting the gloves on and watches me. Red gloves, a troubled look in her eyes. I feel uncomfortable and stand up as if to leave, trying thus to speed up the process of communication. She says: "I'm looking hard because I feel like painting the walls the color of bull's blood. This wallpaper is horrible, it's gloomy." (I think: she's trying to justify the spots on her hands, her gloves, her attitude.) I fall into the trap anyway and say: "But everything would be red then. You'll be swallowed up by red: the bedspread, the rug, the curtains, the lampshade that casts a red glow over everything. If you want something cheerful, paint the walls white." "Cheerful? You think so?"

I know I should leave. She'll give me nothing more of herself. As my hand rests on the door latch, she hands me a sheet of paper typed on both sides, single spaced. It's like a gift and I'm surprised: so far I've only seen things written by hand and haven't managed to get her to show them to me. She says: I love visits on Tuesdays at midnight. Till next Tuesday, at the stroke of midnight."

As the door shuts behind me I know that on Tuesday I'll arrive for the first time as a guest and I decide to file the sheet of paper she gave me under the heading *Proof I*. I'll read it later. I've already gone down a few steps and she sticks her head out on the landing and whispers: "Be careful at night. It's not made for those who are searching." I run up the stairs three at a time. "Don't thieves and murderers come out at night and search?" "No, they're the ones who show true scorn—the ones really admired."

And she shuts the door in my face.

Mondays and Thursdays, in the wee hours of the morning. Behind the bars of her own eyelashes—the alert semicircular prison of her eyes—Beatriz used to lie waiting for her husband to leave, snoring from a sense of helplessness and out of an inexplicable need to make him think she was asleep. His footsteps leaving the bed, the bedroom, the house, echoed in her tense body, and she knew he was going out on a mission, not on a spree. A man who's out for a good time has another look in his eyes, smells different. He needed a little pain and Beatriz was wise enough to let him writhe.

It was the middle of summer with nights as thick as flies' milk. And he was not the type to go out in August, in the mist, to have a good time. He needed a beacon, a channel marked with buoys, and if he was prepared to navigate through the heat, there was no doubt that his mission was larger than himself. Mondays and Thursdays he slipped out and was back by two: this regularity gave his outings an air of austerity. September came, then October, and Beatriz hadn't really worried or been upset until that night of unprecedented heat, a red night. He muttered some vague excuse and dashed out. It was eleven-thirty, and a Tuesday; there was the smell of rancid cooking oil and fried fish, and the din from the neighbor's radio. For the first time Beatriz was worried: the break in the routine, in the established rules produced a burning in the pit of her stomach. He wouldn't come back, something he could scarcely admit, something hard for his organism to assimilate—an organism not particularly sensitive to the temperature of others. It wasn't something simple, but a danger involved in innocence: the worst of evils.

There is a time for everyone to tremble. It was now the turn of Beatriz the snorer, the sleep pretender, and it is hard to tell whether she's trembling for him or herself. Is she trembling out of love or selfishness? The motives don't change the result:

sweating hands, the urge to scream, the bursting into helpless tears. Meanwhile he's wandering about the tortuous streets, making more twists and turns than a spinning top, than a pig's tail, than life. Life? If he doesn't mind gambling it away on a simple, supposedly scientific caprice—and as a matter of fact he doesn't —under what pretense can he enter the lives of other men/ women? Too much to ask of a mortal who is not unaware of his human condition. Too much to ask for and if one asks too much, as a rule one gets everything one asks for but with no time to enjoy it, and on to another thing (which is sometimes the same thing but with a subtle difference: a lack of desire).

•

I like following him with my finger on the map of the city and sometimes going with him. I like nighttime: night is another country, a chest of mirrors, a nest of sparrows, night is the possibility of entering through the other door, it's floods of tears with consolation enclosed, the night is being inside oneself. I like following him with my finger on the map of this city or another, he likes to hurry down filthy alleyways and know where he's going, the idea of losing him worries Beatriz, but not the other woman: on this Tuesday at midnight she waits in peace, thinking that a little death is worth the other death.

•

Other voices often criticize and complain:

"This woman doesn't want us to live our own lives she disturbs us she doesn't let us sleep peacefully in bed she isn't like other women. Not that she makes strange noises or she prowls the rooftops." (Why does he mention prowling the rooftops? There were times when this did attract her, but in the sunlight when she was a little girl and to no special purpose. She didn't spy on people down below, she merely swung on the cornices, ran silently over the rooftops and slid down to the adjoining terraces, farther and farther away from her own house, until she reached the heart of the block. She discovered treasures: the rooftops are a source of unsuspected delight with chimneys that aren't made for anyone's eye and statues hidden amid climbing plants. She had wandered over the rooftops, it's true, but not now, not now. Not now. What were the neighbors complaining about anyway?)

"It's true, believe me, we can't sleep knowing she's so close because she's got—what shall I say?—a pair of eyes: eyes that radiate light, that make noise, eyes that you don't see or touch but always know are there; you can smell them, you can hear them behind the walls, those eyes, it's as if they were looking for something, they scrutinize you, they search your insides. Can you tell me what could be hidden in my lung, in my liver, or behind my ear? She looks at us and searches, and we feel dirty when she's the dirty one, goddammit, not because we have anything against an activity that's old and socially necessary, but no one can say that prostitution is purity. I've hung around with them a lot and still do, and I'm telling you prostitutes can be good girls, even hard-working, but you can't say they're saints, no sir, they know how much vice they're responsible for. But not her, she walks down the streets, climbs the stairs, goes down the corridors just like anybody else, like a virgin pure and clean.

Once my wife was screaming because she said she had seen a black cat with splinters in its eyes coming out her window. I looked and saw a black cat, all right, but one without any slivers in its eyes, a nice healthy cat though kind of skinny, slinking along the cornice. I'm not saying that she tortures animals or anything like that, though she may well do so, who knows, but that's the atmosphere she creates around her. Poor ordinary people like us start imagining things, that she has powers, and though I'm not about to listen to the local gossip I know that women have nothing to do with this: poor idiots, they don't even know how to make things up: she's the one who prompts it all, who instills fear in people. This was a neighborhood without fear before she got here. I don't say it was a quiet neighborhood because, well, you know it better than I do and it wasn't quiet and never will be: there are quarrels, an occasional knifing, problems with fags, and all that. But those were things that had an explanation, they weren't scary. With her here the air is hard to breathe and we don't feel this is our house any more. What does she eat anyway? We've never seen her at the market or in the grocery store or any place else where you buy food. She must eat things other than food, and she must really need them so as to poison the minds of those other girls. They don't deliver the way they used to, they've grown lazy, bad-tempered. They've gotten together, they're demanding social security and an eight-hour work day. As if lying in bed having fun wasn't the most restful work in the world. I've always looked out for them, I've insisted that they bring their customers to the rooms I rent out in the back of the house: I keep an eye out for them, I protect them and give them running water besides. And you see how they thank me, the ungrateful little bitches—by forming a union! She's a witch I tell you, she's poisoned their minds. The Inquisition is what we need, somebody with a heavy hand to deal with her. The other day I saw her with a bunch of cards in her hand and I assure you it wasn't to play poker. She has several wooden owls in her room that she was going to send to someone for some spooky reason. All the girls in the neighborhood listen to her because she's bewitched them and before long it won't be safe for us men: they'll be tossing us out into the street, they'll be yanking our cocks off. That must be what she eats—men's most vital parts. Yes, I spy on her, I do, and in the small hours of the morning I see a man like yourself coming to her place, never the same one, and leaving dead tired. She must suck his blood, leave him just enough strength to stagger out of her place and die like a dog. Where do you think all those strangers who turn up dead around here come from? From my house, sir, from the farthest little corner of the garret, but from my house. I curse the day I rented that room, and I had a bath put in and all to get someone decent, and she uses the basin to wash her hands after the butchery and to rinse out her mouth. She must castrate men with her teeth. Those foolish girls refuse to understand that by destroying men night after night she destroys their source of work. They now demand to work only certain hours and not exceed a certain number of jobs per week. And I'm tired of explaining to them that she's talking them into it so they won't notice that business is falling off. Every night, for lack of virility or life, there are fewer and fewer clients, and it's all her doing. The girls laugh in my face, they insult me, call me a sly old fox. She's bewitched those girls into believing they're somebody, they think they're human beings, and I broke my back teaching them the tricks of the trade. They think they're big shots, they talk about meetings and a strike. A strike, for crying out loud! They make me laugh. Can you picture the city if the whores stopped working? It's that woman's fiendish work. And some of them even say she's from the same country as me. She must be, to be such a bitch."

Second Complaint

The worst of it is that sometimes she looks nice even though she's ugly and not so young. The worst of it is that she doesn't look bad at all.

Third Complaint

The worst of it is that she exists.

don't let me escape, don't let me act, don't let me do a thing. tied hand and foot is the way I feel best, gagged and blindfolded, please don't let me move, my lips sewn shut, my eyelids too, my fingers are swollen. my fingers have a will of their own and I want to stop them. sighs escape me. there are movements deep inside my body. I'm standing up now with my five senses in my hand and I intend to make my sense of touch the supreme master, standing up without looking ahead, moving in rhythm. the silence is far from being what matters most to me but it has its attractions, its unfulfilled desires; the silence is one of us. let him alone, I want to see him dance. let him alone and he'll have his turn in today's great dance. to make him dance the way he should I'll put a red-hot poker to his feet and he'll lift first the one and then the other to rhythms I dictate. let him alone because otherwise you'll get fried like moths that get too close to the light. not approaching the light takes a form of courage, since keeping in the shadows benefits no one. I'm sad and I don't know who to blame now that all the guilty parties are on vacation. vacations of guilty parties—they deserve them. taking the blame is tiring, lots of people can prove what I'm saying.

not me. I don't feel guilty because I haven't done any harm. I'm good, I generously forgive anything he asks me to, I'm a fountain of forgiveness and I deal it out lavishly. I love them all and want to console them, that's why I caress them; I begin by caressing them with my voice, then with my breath, then I caress them with my hands and finally with my deepest and most hidden being. I give them everything I have and consolation besides; he too gets everything from me, everything I force him to have. Outside the regular hours, outside of time is when I love him best, when I claw at him the most. I have only a minute to vent my fury, like the fireworks at the fair, then nothing. The big bang, like a bomb going off, and he'll suddenly burst into a thousand colors, he'll be himself and a thousand more, and he'll go far away from me when he tries to get close to me. I've got him now, I must devour him skin and all, and then on to something else, some other damnation.

It's good to follow him through the streets at midnight like a wily dog, to climb the stairs and wind down the long corridors and then lie in wait at her door while she makes up her mind. It's good to nap a while, dreaming of the smell of his heels, to wake up when I hear him shouting, to scratch lightly on the door and go on hoping. It's good to hear him screaming again —screams are of pleasure or of agony—and to accompany him with howls and know that outside there's a full moon and he's probably letting himself be clawed to death by her. Until the final bang.

Beatriz is a skinny animal, Beatriz is a starving, toothless animal and is afraid as she waits for him to come home, bumping into the walls because the extent of her night watch is greater than the space available. The limits of the house don't match the limits of her body, and now and then a murmur like a howl escapes her. The walls press in on her, the walls gradually hem her in, close around her, imprison her, and Beatriz knows that she cannot run through the streets at night because that is her husband's domain and she's afraid to invade it, to break the rules. The walls are closing in on Beatriz, while for the other woman they are a different universe:

the walls don't creak now because nobody is forcing them from the inside. they are solid, that's for sure, though a few cracks show through which the water could escape if they were the walls of a dike. the bellies of dikes are as immeasurable as Gothic cathedrals. I've been in the belly of dikes, in the heart of the roaring waters, but this part of my story I prefer to keep to myself (because I didn't dare put the bomb in the right place?). anything can happen inside walls and I'm not ready to expose myself as I am but only as I'd like to be, pitiless and cynical, clenching my teeth to prevent even the slightest gush of sentiment. no room for pity here. or for mercy. then I can express myself as I please and not dread the green, sticky substance that is fear. it will take long years of sacrifice for me to reach the point I desire, but *today I pull the trigger to announce that I'm clearing out, that I'm giving the coup de grâce.*

he and I get into a coach drawn by four white horses and on their backs the coachman draws maps of blood with his whip (the coachman draws on their backs maps of blood with his whip on their backs the coachman draws maps of blood with his whip the coachman with his whip draws maps of blood on their backs), the scene is repeated once more and makes me shiver. I yell at the coachman, I pull the trigger, and he falls dead—he, not the coachman. usually my aim is poor.

I shake him furiously, I kiss the wounds, he's stretched out on my bed bleeding, he resembles someone I've loved, but even so I don't know what his name is, not that it matters. I shake him furiously, I tear him apart, I have an arm in my hand, a hand in my hand, a head in my hand. he doesn't interest me any more: he's come apart like all of them, all men are alike, they don't hold up.

It's six o'clock in the morning and he hasn't come back, says Beatriz as she files her fingernails. I'll go mad.

It's nine o'clock and he's still not back, says Beatriz as she plucks her eyebrows. I'm just a little crazy.

It's noon and he couldn't even take the trouble to telephone. I think I'll scream.

                (it's a known fact that madness advances one step every 3 hours)

The mirror sends her back the reflection of her worn out face. The mirror sends it back to her, thank you. Meanwhile she looks at herself looking for herself, searching for the other face of the coin, the face of the other woman who must be somewhere, for heaven's sake, in some corner of this damn city there must be a woman who swallowed her husband alive and with his tail wagging, maybe not quite wagging but certainly alive, more alive than ever even though she's liquidated him. She swallowed him, leaving to her (to Beatriz, his lawful wife) a certain taste of him still lingering in her mouth. A belch.

As if it were easy to do something to him and it is. He's much more fragile than meets the eye, and more vulnerable. Beatriz knows just how vulnerable he is and so at times she attacks/ attacked him. She can't now, not even this quiet haven is left her to enjoy. He will not come back, his body has perhaps grown cold in the arms of some other woman, O horror, O cruel and pitiless fate that has wrenched him from my arms. I can no longer press him to my bosom. What crime have I committed against heaven to make me pay in this bloody manner for my modest share of happiness? Even though it's with his blood that I pay my debts to destiny, O cruel, O intransigent fortune. He's paying for my fears, for everything reproachable in me. They are showing him to me—no, I don't want to see him, I don't want to see him shedding the blood that was mine briefly at least, I don't want to see him with a bullet hole in his left temple or a dagger sticking out of his belly. He must be a sight, hemmed in like that, why must his body be so far away from me, cold though it be? I would know how to appreciate the esthetics of his post-mortem state, to appreciate, to applaud infamies, if I were allowed to play too.

Bea laughs as she looks at herself in the mirror, she stops enjoying the melodrama and is lost in thought. And at 3:15 p.m. on Wednesday he enters with faltering footsteps and a more or less guilty look on his face. Thorns above the whiteness of a shroud and dark circles under his eyes. The face of Lazarus; at least that was the way Bea saw it.

The regulations don't say what steps to take when your husband comes home reeling after a night of carousing and you've spent your time worrying and thinking him dead in a sewer. The regulations have come down to us in a somewhat incomplete form and you mustn't think that reactions just happen; Bea tried out three—hate, scorn, and grief—but got no response from this man who was wiped out from having fought for his life for fifteen hours. It doesn't sound like much when you put it that way and think that in the usual course of events you fight for your life all your life, but he'll explain to her that it's not the same. Facing death is one thing, remote control is quite another. He survived the game head on and feels like a hero half dead with fatigue. Let us therefore respect the warrior's respite even though he fought against nothing, or rather surrendered in the various forms that she demanded of him from the moment he arrived in her garret until the stifling noon when, somewhat transformed, he left it. The tables are turned—the boomerang effect or, if you prefer, going for wool and coming out fleeced. Last night he needed a helping hand, she gave him a kick in the face and said I'm helping you; or maybe it was the reverse:

she tried to help him and accidentally kicked him, or she thought that kicking him was a form of help, or better still she didn't help him or kick him but he believed that it was one or the other or both. The help is in the kick and vice versa: you have to be something of a masochist to allow other people to come to an understanding with you. In any event he acted courageously and only fainted twice, close to the end of the odyssey. One wonders how many times she would have fainted if she had followed him (this is false too, to detract from her merits out of envy: she not only followed him and at times even preceded him along the way, but also there is ample reason to believe that she was the one responsible for the trip). The result: his return home at three in the afternoon with circles under his eyes, to find Bea laughing in front of the mirror though not at all happy or out of her head but merely surprised, and his discovery that you can't underestimate women (a woman)—they're all equally hermetic and outrageous.

And so he caressed Bea's face in the mirror and said:

My darling, you mustn't mistrust me. Everything I do, have done, or will do outside this house is to gain knowledge. Not *inside* the house. Here I do things for pleasure pure and simple. Outside that door, my beloved, the demon of my calling overtakes us and we must make our way to certain shadowy creatures who require our analysis. The study of these creatures robs me of hours of sleep, it gnaws at my vitals, gives me no rest; the knowledge that this is a noble task which someday will benefit the entire human race, and in particular the person that I'm analyzing, impels me to go on in spite of the sacrifices. That, my beloved, is why I've spent this long period without sleep, let's say a night, outside the sweet refuge of my home and fireside. For the sake of science, needless to say, and it's to the credit of science too that this refreshing sleep that I'm about to submit to will redound. So kindly don't disturb me until dinnertime. Got it?

. . .

Bea understood quite a few things even before he woke up and told her of his outside life, admittedly with only a few details, and covering only a few of the recent nights despite their having been so innocent and so much commented upon, a pure blablabla creeping up the walls (red, you say?) until it covered everything including the two of them.

Bea was well informed regarding the tragic night, or rather somewhat well informed since he took care not to tell her about all his adventures. He did of course reveal a few details sewn together with big stitches, so that what Bea needed to know to complete the story had nothing to do with the story he wasn't able to tell her—his exhausting session in bed with her the night before, submerged in a quite unexpected passion and tenderness that might have lasted indefinitely had not the damned clock struck three. She knew that the time had come and leaped up —no, she wasn't sleeping, she was watching his every move, the least of his whims, so as to make love to him better. (Why do you have such big eyes, such eager lips, such a moist tongue? Why are you alive? The better to eat you, my son.) And he knew that she knew, and at that point she knew that he knew that she knew, and it didn't seem to make a bit of difference. Everything would continue as before, with obscure disguises and obscure pretenses, because it wasn't a question of hiding the simple and inevitable fact of having a gentleman sufficiently interested in one's life to come a long distance twice a week at late hours juggling a thousand masks, but rather of forgetting the last little detail, of leaving aside the other life that never can be told to a third party—of changing skin, changing skin, changing skin as many times as necessary.

It was precisely at three A.M., with the revelation that she had never been fooled by his disguises, that he began to be afraid. Not before, not even when under the pillow he felt the little .32 with the pretty mother-of-pearl inlays.

She on the other hand was a virgin where fear was concerned, but what began to penetrate her was something else: an indefinable suspicion that perhaps he (an Argentine, forty-three, presumably married and with children, monogram AZ on his shirt, a professor of semiotics—?!—at the University of Barcelona, name not determined out of indifference) was an agent of the Army Intelligence, Interpol, or the CIA, sent with the sole purpose of pumping her for information that she was not only disinclined to give but considered irrelevant. One's own life can be narrated only if (a) it does not involve others; (b) it does not stoop to mere anecdote; (c) one can retouch it *a piacere*. That is why she was prepared once more, in an opening and closing of her legs, to give everything of herself that essentially belonged to him—that which in one form or another might give him pleasure. And if that displeased him, so much the worse; she was prepared to confront such a contingency, and well armed: a .32, small but sure.

From among an infinite number of ways to catalogue the human species I propose two: those who flee women like her and those who, like me, desperately seek them out. At times it's difficult to recognize such beings, one needs more than a good sense of smell, wisdom, and intuition: one needs a great inner receptivity to see what is there, a *satori* almost, and then suddenly the person in front of us, the one we've lived with for so many years, turns out to be one of them. Professor Weisstern called them mutants, Professor Weisstern ended up being devoured by them as he deserved to be. His mutants were not as cool as mine, they were not professionals at love.* But it is mutants who open the door to change and in some obscure, inexplicable fashion prove to be exceptions to the rules. My scientific mind leads me to search for beings like her, and to make painful attempts to take them apart. But no one can say that I approached her without humility, without zeal. I called into play the passions at my disposal and I'm prepared to pick up the threads of the scandal.

And now, miraculously, my enthusiasm for this investigation has proved catching and I have passed it on to Beatriz. Without of course allowing her to ask too many questions. She's unbeatable as a secretary: carefully and devotedly she helps me to keep my files up to date and to transcribe the tapes. Sometimes she

* She chose love as she might have chosen hatred, with an equal lack of scruples. Doesn't she praise the work of assassins and thieves? Contaminated by literature, she chose the city where Jean Genet lived for a number of years.

even gets up at night when I'm getting ready to go see her, and lays out my costume or combs a new false beard that I've acquired. I never ask her if she's jealous. Fresh, blonde, clean as she is, she can't even feel that she's competing with such an obscure being. Even so I found her crying in the bathroom one morning, and I noticed that she was lost in thought—Bea of all people, who has never been much given to reflection.

Also one night, apparently unintentionally, Bea spilled a few drops of her perfume on my suit just as I was about to go out. On another night, when she appeared with a blonde wig just like her own hair, and insisted that I again play the part of a transvestite—an elegant one this time, dressed in her best evening gown—everything was clear to me. But these are minor incidents, compared with how well she does my transcription work and keeps my files.

But her reaction was strange. The night I arrived at her place in Bea's clothes, she said to me, "I am made to awaken in others a love so intense and real that afterward they cannot bear it and abandon me." Bea smiled as she copied down this sentence, a sad smile, and asked me if there were any notes to add. I said no, because in fact I didn't have any. *She* had come out with that sentence in the middle of a conversation that had nothing to merit it.

I'm a timid man of moderate habits and very few needs. And here you have the timid man of moderatehabitsandveryfewneeds living a double life, not because one life is hidden from the other though there is some of that, but because what he calls his life, the daily routine that takes him to his classroom at the university and makes him study and awakens his interest, has been cut in two. On the one hand there is the man who goes along, who does and undoes, and on the other hand a very different man who mulls over his memories and lives vicariously by digging and scratching around to put himself in somebody else's skin. That of another woman, to cap it all—a woman who stays closed up in her room without making too many concessions to the world, and with her inner burden intact, crying out for someone to poke about in her experiences, to give them back their color.

At times, as I walk down the dark alleyways that lead to her lair, I feel demoniacal; sometimes I hear voices and feel as if I were trying to take possession of her, to devour her, to incorporate her within myself and keep her intact. We must see whether this passion isn't transitive, if it isn't she who's trying to get inside me and possess me. One more reason for worry and research. I ought to note this down but I prefer to keep silent, I don't want Bea or my students to know of my fears, they are innocent, I don't want to pollute them with my horrors.

On a certain night I must have passed on the word fear to *her*. I believe it was before she spoke to me of murderers or mentioned their names. (I'm losing track of the chronological order —time is far from important when the successive nights become one big night and the search is for something that transcends individuals.) On a certain night, I repeat, I arrived in full dress, with a top hat and white gloves. I thought I was a gentleman coming from the Teatro Liceo after an evening at the opera, but as I went up the stairs to her place I thought about Raffles and that's precisely what I must have seemed like, for after a while she began to talk to me of her nighttime fears in her parents' house. Recurrent dreams of two-headed eagles on the terrace to which I may or may not return later on, and above all a confused story about a grandfather clock which she lets me transcribe now because it may have something to do with the episode we were talking of before. (Who's infecting whom with obsessions? She is the great contaminator, she infects the very air she breathes, she says silly things.)

if the ballast prevents you from going up to the stars you'll stay below forever and learn to say excuse me in a loud voice and a soft voice. the soft voice is a substitute for delirium, it's a paranoid word for the vile creatures that know nothing of ignorance, who are unaware of the inner juice of words. I am now on the reverse side of things seeing that side is no fun at all. so I keep running toward the darkest corners of the house and the house is big and has stone corridors and at the end of the corridors is a grandfather clock that sometimes strikes unexpectedly and most of the time remains threateningly silent readying a snake in its belly that would die at the appointed hour if only we knew what hour, if only we had the courage to go beyond the clock and get to the door. the door is narrow, of wood as heavy as the world, and it has four huge nails. we don't like doors that are crosses, that tell us about martyrdom, we only like doors that we cannot find there, transparent doors, slightly frosted, because we know through an experience beyond confession that behind transparent doors there is love, genuine love. but we have strength enough to confront a lack of love down long corridors. we don't have, though, any interest in finding out if the hour has come. the clock can't keep quiet at night, its ticks stretch out along the opaque skin of the house. it has mosaics, the house I mean, everything is ready for the departure that one of the opponents must face at the end of the game. the one that loses will have to leave the house and that's simple: the long corridors are there waiting for him, the clock is there, normal-looking but with an evil disposition. and I am there beginning to play and maybe I lose, maybe I'm the one who has to leave the house. it's not a bad idea after all to take a tumble into the unknown, to lose in order to get out, and maybe even come out a winner.

outside it's daylight. if I had known that daylight existed maybe I would have started playing earlier. but I don't know what those inside might do if the loser of the game refuses to leave. I think, I suspect, and I've heard tell that they're capable of anything, of more than one can conceive and the stomach take. I personally have been consistently forgetting resentments and I want them to play for the pleasure of a good game in which there are no winners and no losers. if they knew something of pleasure it would be easy to persuade them. but they refuse to indulge in this type of sophistication—good digestion, complete satisfaction is beyond them. if they were satisfied they wouldn't be good for anything, but that's their business, they feel like martyrs for the simple reason that they're in catacombs. I never found out what feeling like a martyr was all about but I tried reluctantly to imitate them. It turns out that being a martyr isn't as simple as it seems, there must be more to seeing what doesn't exist and absolutely refusing to bow to the evidence. now that the game is lost and I'm outside I've forgotten a whole lot of their habits, I've forgotten how they spend their nights for example, I don't know if they have a rhythmical awareness or if they act on a whim. will they respect the few hours that strike on the clock in the background? will that same clock always strike the same hours or is it unpredictable? besides I don't know if the snake in the clock exists but I fear it doesn't. for them the imaginary monsters are much more fierce than those waiting their turn. I'm out now and I don't know if I can bear it, if I'm not dying for them, I'd rather be inside feeling their imaginary warmth. sometimes I walk all through the house and fail to find a single little window to remind me of what's inside there. at times I feel about with my hands in search of a tiny crack, but the walls are solid and won't take pity on anybody. these walls: not a single chink so I can find out something about my brothers inside. from the outside the house is like a cube of cement and to think that inside it seemed so broad and narrow. there must be a thousand rooms shut off, any number of secret rooms—and I can't tell them so—rooms that perhaps contain the truth we're searching for, rooms where perhaps they've locked up the light that's in everybody's mind though nobody mentions it. I know now that it's not the light of day we're searching for, I know now that it's another level of reality. the sun, the sun has nothing to do with our struggle unless we happen to be looking for an archaic sun, a sun inside of us.

leaving the search without knowing what's being sought is not pleasant. I now see the sun, the moon, the stars and I know that it's not from any of these natural sources that the light we're searching for comes, the light that lives in shadows.

Bea wonders why the other woman says what she says and above all why she thinks as she does. She wonders and will continue to wonder if her husband isn't giving her some drug to make her so lucid and at the same time so obscure. (We're trying to see through her opaque body, one of these days we might get a piece of information, a revelation that will make us understand a great deal or at least explain why we are suffering on her account without any apparent benefit.) He's no longer the same, I'm different too, in this house someone intrudes on our hours and kills everything it touches. My skin has turned gray, one by one the fish in the aquarium have died, the flowers have faded, the plants in their pots have dried up.

Bea realizes that this is merely a fantasy and she can do nothing to make it go away. She can't even take to her bed and phone the doctor and ask him to change her anxieties. A little bit of the drug that her husband is giving the other woman would probably do her good; she searches for some all over the house, in his pockets, but there's nothing. He denies the existence of any strange drug, he says that natural phenomena still are the most difficult to explain.

He is on time for their rendezvous at three in the morning. They behave as if they didn't expect each other. She is dressed in a peasant dress and has long curls while he is dressed in a sailor suit: an old salt with a beard and no mustache, a striped T-shirt, and a bag over his shoulder, and for a fleeting moment she fantasizes that he might carry her away to the here-place, the place of forgetfulness. He ought to do that for once, he ought to show a little courage.

His needs are not so much physical, he merely tries to imprint on the air the idea of traveling, to leave it floating in the air so that she'll finally remember her far-off native land and talk of their first meeting. (Even though she might say it was with someone else. Surely she'll say it was with someone else, but what did he care, he'd recognize himself among a thousand shadows, his appearance of fifteen years ago would show up clearly in her words and he'd know what to expect.)

And she persists in nonremembering, not anything. And he tries to press her, which finally results in a night of little interest, few vibrations.

I'm afraid of being only a ghost in the memory of certain gentlemen who find it pleasant to busy themselves with me but can't bear my presence for long. for some of them I'm only a speck of pepper stuck between their teeth; much later they bite down without thinking and there I am burning their tongue and I don't even rate an insult.

I would have to sniff this sentence up, down, and sideways, hold it up to the light and look through it, try to discover if anything of myself is caught in it—I who indeed was left with a grain of pepper bigger than a house and now that the time for biting has come I feel my tongue, my mouth, my entire person burning, blazing like fire. But I shouldn't worry about that intrusion of mine on other levels of life: she's a valid subject for study, a rare example, so I must concentrate on my work and not allow myself to be distracted by prior events beside the point. Whether or not she's the same as fifteen years ago has little to do with that moment when she stood out from the crowd in the Plaza Real and was pointed out to me as a subject for my investigation—her analysis.

I regret not having someone in this city capable of checking my work. At times I panic and think with horror that I'm using her as a mirror, putting on masks in order to see myself better, expecting her to send back my real image. I must know, I want to know.

It's hard to untie this knot. What she really wants to hide is of no importance to him, it could interest him only if there were some remote possibility of his joining the cause. But here in Barcelona she knows there's no hope of that, it's a safe refuge for hiding one's miseries. A forced exile for political reasons that we'll forget here and now, and a cowardly escape for reasons of love that she'd like to forget forever.

But the man had a name, Alfredo Navoni, plus a number of aliases that will come out as this tale unfolds if in fact it unfolds. This one she prefers to keep nameless and with many faces, so as not to have to love him or suspect him of anything.

Time with Navoni was more real (a reality only in appearance as always happens. Chronological time of the kind we have in our lives, measurable, with cracks for hope, chance, good intentions, all that may turn against one). She had her universe then and a lover enrolled in the guerrilla forces who went underground and forgot her.

So many thousands of kilometers to get away from this. Such attention devoted to creating the fortress of nights and disguises and indifference and death when all of a sudden the intruder enters the picture (the voyeur, the kibitzer, the impartial observer, the meddler), and after countless careful efforts he slips in some remark regarding the other experience, the time before, the past that should be wiped away, crossed out with a stroke of a pen because it's useless. And she again unraveling, languishing, so as to remember, if only once more, part of those times. And the images return as if sketched under threat. Repulsive.

She was able to detect the first sign of the hateful infiltration the night she told him the two dreams of Alfredo Navoni—alias the Tiger—as if they were her own. Who could have told her of those two dreams of Navoni's? Not Navoni, no, for they stripped him naked by revealing his passion for her, his most jealously kept secret. On the other hand he dreamed them in Formosa in fever and delirium, on a mission that was not successful and he ended up in jail. They were dreams to be dismissed out of hand, but she told them as though they were her own.

Navoni's two dreams

1. Love hunger
In a distant city there lives a man who is in love with me. But as time goes on, love turns into something altogether different. At the beginning he feels the desire to eat me up, to suck all my bones dry, but eventually he feels a real hunger, yum, yum —an uncontrolled, evil animal hunger. To come from his bed to my city he cuts the tiger-skin rug into strips and winds them around himself like a mummy. He can thus go quietly about on all fours and along the way try to get his fangs to grow, so his hunger for me will be genuine and nicely whetted.

In the woods a wolf smells his man odor beneath the tiger skin and attempts to throw himself upon him. But it gets a bullet square in the forehead because the man realizes in the nick of time that his fangs cannot yet compete with those of the wolf.

. . .

The man drinks wolf blood that afternoon, and eats wolf cutlets that night. Grilled, of course, as befits a being that a short while before had been part of so-called civilization. In search of a safe place, he stretches out in the hay of an old barn because he knows that of all wild animals man alone doesn't fear sleeping under a roof, particularly when armed.

The following morning the farm dog approaches, barking and wagging its tail and again barking frantically. Dog and man discover at the same time that his teeth have grown in the night though his lips are still human and tender. On seeing the man's fangs, the dog lets out a howl that the man is able to take up and even go one better, for his own howl is not that of a dog but a wolf.

The man with the fangs looks like a full moon and the dog sits whining, as if hypnotized. Spittle oozes out between the man's fangs and the dog suddenly feels the fangs on his neck and it's too late.

Wolfman and deaddog stay in the barn until the man takes out his knife and skins the dog to make a softer cape than the tiger skin for himself. And he doesn't need to cook the dog's flesh in order to eat it, all he has to do is rub it on the cows' salt lick.

He finally comes out under cover of darkness the way wild beasts do and slinks through the woods till he reaches the river. He flops on his stomach to lap up water and feels a freshness that warms him until his insides burn. He howls.

The river has turned hot, steam rising off it, but he must continue to move along the river so the dogs can't smell his tracks. The enormous effort of wading through the dense water makes his hunger for me still greater, and he travels night and day enveloped in the steam, following meanders that don't always lead to my place, that sometimes take him farther away. I am in despair because I can't call him to tell him to get to me and to eat me.

He has digested the dog flesh fast, and more than once he must leave the protection of the river to look for a duck's nest amid the fields of tall grass. He wrings the neck of the first duck he comes across, plucks it, and eats it, taking care to cast the innards aside. He kills the second duck and plucks it while its wings are still flapping. He is eating greedily when he hears a cock crow in the distance. He abandons the remains of the duck and runs so that dawn won't surprise him in the midst of a mutation.

2. Railroad striptease
In this dream I see myself through the eyes of a man who unexpectedly arrives at a railroad gate that I know of, half hidden in my city. The gate is down and the man who is my eyes has to stop his car and wait with the windows shut tight because it's cold. It's an incredible night and the branches hide the one light in the trees, letting only a yellow sliver through when the wind stirs the leaves. The man looks through the misty windshield and suddenly sees me coming down the railroad tracks, dragging along a heavy table. I stop opposite the gate, I measure precisely where the middle of this section of the track is, and place the table between two tracks. I hardly recognize myself because I look more like a polar bear, I'm wrapped in a great fur coat and have a fur cap on my head. But I—the man, my eyes—know that I'm myself and that I'm cold and that the man wants to get out of the car to embrace me but my eyes prefer just to watch.

The bundle of clothes that's me on the other side of the gate clambers up onto the table as best it can and begins to move slowly to the rhythm of a harsh music that emanates from inside it. Then in slow, deliberate movements it takes off its cap, wool gloves, cap, wool gloves, heavy shoes. A striptease in due and proper form except that the garments are ordinary and unerotic. The music that comes out of me grows more passionate, the air is filled with recorded sighs. A thick ski sock hits the windshield and I go on slowly writhing, taking off my sweater slowly, slowly, until I'm standing there in my bra, facing straight ahead and a gleam grows brighter on my breasts and then the roar of the train is heard, louder and louder till it drowns out the music and the recorded sighs. In his eyes I am in despair, I am still fearlessly standing on the table, I take off my panties, I writhe to the same rhythm, the gleam grows brighter yet, the roar gets louder, I caress my hips and begin to untie the ribbons of my bikini top and the light becomes blinding and just as I'm about to take off the bikini the train is there on top of me and I see myself fly into a thousand colored flashes brighter than fireworks.

Why so much effort, after all? Telling and hiding and refusing to associate and then hoping in anguish that another Thursday will come and then again the fear that he'll be bored and never come back. And for what? For something that she seeks, leaning now against the little Gothic window, hidden behind the red velvet curtain in the glow of the red lamp that creates a particular atmosphere, an aura of desire, of purity.

Looking for purity now seems pretentious on her part, and it is: hers is a highly contaminated inner world that makes her fascinating but not at all transparent.

He and Bea realized that there were more things hidden in her life than was possible to imagine, not after she told those two dreams but later. Perhaps when the word *sister* crossed her lips, even though she was being careful but not careful enough to avoid a certain inflection, a certain tone in her voice that gave away the game of flawed mirrors that send back the image of some other (wo)man. There she was. Closed in. Prepared to keep to herself the charge too electric for a lonesome woman. She vanished during the day and no one ever saw her in the Pasaje des Escudellers in the street of the same name or in the Plaza Real which might have pleased her with palm trees that reminded her of her South America. (What was it like for her in Latin America? What tricks can she have learned there, what misery?) Misery does not have a miserymeter to measure it, hence we cannot determine how much of it there is in her or decide on the dosage or write the proper prescription.

The most reasonable course would be to leave her in peace contemplating or denying her memories, giving up consolation, giving up memories of dialogues including consolation, of times when she and her twin sister, or she-she as she used to call her (the two of them so identical, so nicely counterbalanced, so analogous and simultaneous and conscious and ductile), used to fight for the same cause and even found a way to have hope. Not later, no, trapped as they had been, tortured and humiliated. The impossibility then of doing anything for others and the need for the great break. Losing sight of her sister, of the group, in order to find herself. The need to forget in order to pull oneself together. Forgetting the struggle, forgetting ideals which afterward were trampled on, stained. The need to escape was enormous, to escape from herself, to get out of her badly wounded skin, to forget the love of Alfredo Navoni not knowing if he was the traitor who finally turned them in to the police. To grow a tougher hide, tough enough to survive failure and also pull herself together.

So forget Alfredo, her sister, and that past too painful to be true, stories invented down to the last detail, even the non-verbalized ones, the details that can be guessed at. At least now she's trying to convince herself that it was all a great collective invention as always happens without anyone being able to determine where one stops inventing and lets someone else take over.

She is in Tepoztlán, Iquitos, Bahía, Cartagena, Valparaiso. So much effort, so many contacts thrown overboard. But this concrete story that she's trying to hide doesn't interest the one who is listening to it. And she, ignorant of what he's up to, leaves her most vulnerable flanks exposed while she's careful to protect her other flanks, alien and sterile. Alien in the sense that the principal role belongs to other (wo)men. Sterile, because even though political passions as well as love affairs are always seeds of the very finest quality, in this case the seeds have matured in the barn, have burst, fermented, and finally been burned up in spontaneous combustion and nothing has happened here.

· · ·

Here, or rather there, to be geographically more precise, something that is almost impossible in her case: geographical precision is as far removed from her considerations as chronological precision.

Mondays after Thursdays after Mondays, and an occasional Saturday when Bea gave in, he could meet her in her garret though the way became sometimes steep. Almost a routine until that Saturday at three in the morning when he rang her doorbell and she didn't hurry to answer because she was in another pose, immersed in another life.

And here in reality, in Barcelona? Reality? What sort of place is that? There's a Barcelona that is and yet is not, the one she encounters when walking the streets because a woman who has lost her name can't go down one street after the other; she can't belong everywhere and nowhere, she can't mislay herself. *And I who am now writing can't keep following her because I have an anchor that ties me down to a single succession of images, I can't slip my moorings, spread myself about, or I would be with her in her inexistence, enjoying the privilege of not belonging while belonging with my entire person. In other words the absolute, diluted here there and everywhere because of the summary power of renunciation.*

She never mentioned her name, he never asked her for it. He didn't want to pigeonhole her, he wanted to leave her free between the walls of her room that was the entire city, that surrounded the world and protected it. She was the guardian of the monsters that he worshipped, that were worshipped by every intrepid explorer crossing the river and going beyond the forest where the human condition is finally deposited. Beyond the path of stone, the path hard to travel, the winding path. And the Andes: they keep a great deal to themselves, they don't tell anybody what they think and she is the guardian of the monsters carved in the rock, writhing stone lizards, the giants with panther fangs, the fierce masks, the double beings, she is the only guardian in the cold night air, the insipid twilight air at the height of the clouds. On the heights everything is the gray color of time and stone, a green moldy with fatigue. She is the guardian of other heights as well which I prefer to erase from her memory in order to begin all over again. Except that beginning all over again can't be done successfully forever, can it? One must accept cycles and allow oneself to be carried along by the current.

He too liked the company of monsters, so he spent the entire afternoon with Gaudí, reassembling the giant iguanas made of plates broken in some silent domestic spat. Everything in Gaudí is peacefully tumultuous, and this city I swear is an inferno where the damned are not respected, where rape takes place at the level of one's eardrums, and the noise that distracts us from our remote, unhealthy thoughts, those malodorous thoughts that each of us cradles within himself. He has spent the afternoon with Gaudí: a homemade bestiary, a walking about streets to give them the curves of meringue. A city dreamed by Gaudí to make a court of miracles proliferate in it: the hunchback with eyes leaping in glee, the legless man laughing like a madman, the two-headed woman and armless children with hands emerging from their necks. (All visions, he realizes with no little horror, prompted by her, since she once confessed to him that the first time she ever saw a little boy naked she looked for his other hand, the third hand that the little boy was hiding between his legs in order to point one finger at her [can it be to efface this accusing sign or to search for something she has lost deep inside her that today she allows fingers, many strong fingers, to poke about her freely?].)*

On arriving home he would have liked to eat and sleep before going on his nocturnal visit, but Bea didn't let him and at three A.M., punctual though exhausted, he arrived at her place and collapsed in the armchair, too weak to ask questions, but instead he listened humbly to her theory which afterward he could calmly analyze in the relative security of his study:

* *Note scrawled at the foot of the page:*
search when there is more time to establish the relation between the first image of the naked male (the little boy) and the statue of San Martín, her love-hate for Buenos Aires and the square in the center of town where the statue is, her early childhood memories when she would tease adults to buy her toy cars so she could seduce little boys (with their clothes on).

. . .

there are too many people in this world and everything is so badly distributed. we ought to be like russian dolls: we ought to fit inside each other and mingle our lives and exchange experiences. I want to be the smallest of the russian dolls, the one that's farthest inside and doesn't open. but I can share in the exchange because I have a good store of memories. sometimes I classify them, I shuffle them and mix them up, I shift the faces about, I reassign the gestures (badly) and even the intentions. like those children's books with the pages cut in three that combine the head of one person and the body of another and the legs of a third. nice, isn't it? the magician's top hat. sometimes I put my hand in and pull out a memory that's still wagging its tail or dripping from the moisture it's preserved in. I can spend days on end dredging up memories, that's why I've traveled so much, gone to the remotest places searching for them. now I have finally found my peace between four walls, putting my hand in and taking out at random. Say a word, just one word and you'll see.

"Radio."

"oh no, damn. it reminds me of my neighbor's radio, the pimp's, blasting away all the time. give me another one that sounds better."

"Hen."

"ah, a black one of course. because we're in maracaibo with milton, obsequious, smiling, booming milton pretending that his pores ooze goodness and angelic peace but what comes out of milton's pores is something else, more like oil and I like his son, so submissive but with such passionate green eyes. milton will officiate at the ceremony, the boy is his acolyte, his slave, and my angel—do you see what my memories are like, how splendid, how generous, how magnanimous? now I'm in the middle of the circle of fire and the flames are converging on me and in my hand I have a little carved skeleton and it's me that milton is exorcising. I need a purification right now I notice, milton says the ritual words that I repeat in a soft voice, he takes the sword out of my hand and gives me a lighted candle, he passes the sword over my head my face my shoulders my breasts my sides my hips my musclesmycalvesbetweenmylegsmyheelmyinstep the soles of my feet that I lift up one after the other I rise up oh milton! my jaw drops the son looks at me with those green eyes of his he puts himself in my mouth he's so quiet he passes down my esophagus my stomach my liver my ovaries my uterus he doesn't go out the same way he came in, meanwhile the black hen has laid an egg and milton's son who's just been born from me is cutting the black hen's head off above my body, his hands have gotten through the circle of fire, milton's hands too, they're unfastening my blouse they're taking it off and smearing my belly with the blood of a black hen so I'll be marked forever. the son is now completely milton's son he isn't mine any more milton is here to help me he caresses me down below he makes all the evil go into my hands where he's deposited the white egg of the black hen which is now lying at my feet like an offering, if only my legs would hold me up, if only my legs were good for something and all of me wasn't shot inside the egg; the look in my eyes is now as crystal clear as water (as milton's son) and the egg is no longer in my hands because it's passed into milton's hands, in my hands is a glass of water as crystal clear as the look in my eyes and milton says to me breathe on the egg and I breathe on the egg, on all the eggs and their allegories, I go beyond them, and when milton breaks the egg into the glass and the yolk and the whites mix with the water forms begin to appear, strange filaments separate from the liquid, it's pantheon dirt, milton says. thorns appear, enormous thorns appear that could never have fit in such a little egg. and all the evil that's been put inside me for so many years remains there in an ex-crystalline glass of water, and I'm clean now and can be here or anywhere else because all my evil—my whole being—has remained behind in a glass of water in the white of an egg in a deserted street on the way to the lake. sounds pretty, doesn't it?" "Pretty but useless," we answer. "Too literary. One doesn't have to wander all over the world storing

memories just for that. Wasting time. All you need do is to invent a little or a lot, stretch out on the bed and begin to dream."
"Stretch out on the bed? Not a bad idea."

(The recording is interrupted here. As she transcribed it my wife heard the click and it attracted her attention but she didn't ask any questions, no doubt thinking it a defect in the tape recorder. It's better for Bea not to know certain things, they are beside the point in an investigation for scientific purposes, but we must learn once and for all that with her—not with Bea, of course, but with *her*—it's best not to utter certain words that are too highly charged. Must we learn, must we give up? These occasional accidents, so to speak, these marginal notes don't turn up in every session but only rarely, and they don't distract us from our intended purpose but rather afford us the possibility of getting to know new facets of her extremely rich personality [so rich in secretions, so moist, so warm].)

Bea heard the click but wasn't able to interpret it (sometimes one lives with a woman a thousand years and yet that woman never understands you); at times one unthinkingly allows an unknown woman to absorb the best of oneself (in a literal way) and this unknown woman—she—suddenly intuits everything, guesses everything, and one is naked in her eyes even though one has only unbuttoned one's pants a little way, as if absentmindedly. She didn't hear the click either not because she was fooling herself like Bea but rather because her attention was not on that barely perceptible bulge in my pocket but on that other much more central bulge constantly increasing in volume thanks to her skillful tongue. However, immediately thereafter, having dried her mouth on my shirt, she went on with her monologue again and talked about recorders with that vivid carnal intuition of hers:

to go from here to there, to travel in the most remote regions is like winding up a time machine or turning on the tape recorder that all of us carry around in our heads. through my travels I tried to erase the old tape and re-record it. but I didn't succeed at all: I could re-record often enough but then again there are recordings that are superimposed, recordings one on top another (the triviality that suddenly attacks me like a punch in the face). I traveled to forget, of course, like everyone else, not to flee as you might think but rather in search of something, I don't know what yet, perhaps a person like yourself but I don't think so. at least I took a step forward by agreeing to the search. except that now I prefer not to budge, I decided not to move for quite a while and that's why I didn't commit a murder that I had all nicely planned, or some other disorder that would force me to leave. I don't want to have to escape in a hurry, I prefer to spend the winter in this room, to imitate winter if necessary, curled up in a corner without necessarily losing out on some nice moment that fate offers me, like the one a little while ago.

(If I didn't erase that *like the one a little while ago* it was because I mistrust my abilities as a collator, and moreover I think Bea will regard this phrase as more of *her* nonsense, more of her babbling.)

What will most disconcert whoever puts the pieces of this puzzle together—or perhaps takes it apart and creates other figures —is the invisible presence of the tape recorder, to which she seemed oblivious. She cannot fail to have noticed it during an embrace, during the few moments of passion they shared, or on patting him when saying good-by, or when he, by some involuntary gesture, started or stopped the little thing. But if she noticed the recorder, she seemed indifferent to the fact that her slightest little sigh was recorded forever. Of course she was careful not to speak of Navoni, of her sister the guerrilla leader, of Adela or Michael. If AZ had known these details he might have interpreted the symbols, deciphered the meaning of her companions in the jail in Formosa (Argentina). He might have interpreted her hatred of her mythical sister, her double, and might even have drawn conclusions. At least he would have been surprised to see all those papers, more than he could imagine. sheet after sheet until you get to the pages that I'm now filling in a crabbed hand, to add to the confusion and complicate this story that the less enlightened claim to see clearly. But if he had had access to certain information, his torture in the end, and perhaps even his death, would have given him a reason for being and that *is intolerable: the cause that justifies the ends, the rational explanation creeping in in the middle of all the irrationality that human conduct implies.*

II. The Loss

Today. I am going. To speak. Of myself. I am going to. Forget her. Abandon her. Put her to one side. Today I am. Tomorrow we will take up again our Duties = her faults. Tomorrow we will return to the Matter under Investigation. Tomorrow we'll be a Mother once again. Let ourselves be sucked. Turned into a Giant Breast. White. How tedious. White. Tedium/terror. Her and her phantoms again. The others. Today: me.

In honor of scientific truth I ought to formulate my first question—do I exist? Exist, that is, in the same intense way as those who weave and unweave the plot of the story.

But this no longer matters to us: the plot or her trying to put us inside the plot. She tried to swallow us up. And so I must give up the study of a character who is not even sincere not to mention whole, and even less in conformity with the norms that rule other beings. Because even if she were duly measured and tabulated and vivisected and recorded, classified, printed, it wouldn't help at all because with her as an example one can never deduce a law that fits her. She is not the rule, she is the exception that doesn't make the slightest effort to prove it but instead destroys it. And so: Good-by.

A day at home
3:00 P.M. A thousand surprises because today everything has
returned to normal, has come once more into the light of day
at AZ's. And the couple are at home in such unusual circumstances, having a good time on the terrace in the nice warm heat
of a feline sun licking their epidermal zones exposed to its soft
caress. In moderate doses ultra-violet rays are beneficial. Nothing overemphasized, everything moderate chez AZ. Everything
nicely weighed again and under control.

The tape recorder has broken down on Bea—either accidentally
or deliberately—and *her* voice no longer echoes in these sur-
roundings.
    "Honeywuggums," Bea says to A. in her best purr. "Itums'
greeny-weeny face no pleasy-weasy me; when itums is roasty-
toasted by the sun itums be more appetizing."
    "Okey-dokey," he answers.
    "Did you like your face greeny-weeny? Did itums feel more
intwesting that way?"
    "Nein, nein."
    "Did itums turn palesy-walesy for her?"
    "NO."

5:30 P.M. Bea, the gentle dove, is serving tea without interrupt-
ing the idiotic conjugal dialogue:
    "Does my wee birdie-wirdie want anovver piece of toasty-
woasty?"
    "Mumpf."
    "Shall I put some nice mammylade on it for itums?"
    "Yum, yum."
    "Itums is going to be so handsome when itums is fed and
doesn't have any nasty-wasty circles under itums' eyes any more.
Maybe itums want to hurry over to her house afterward?"
    "NO."

. . .

9:45 P.M. Tenderly holding hands watching television. Beatriz
takes advantage of the commercials to ask:
"Are you thinking of her?"
"NO!"

10:10 P.M. They sit down at the table, with a good appetite
again.
11:00 P.M. Settled down in his favorite chair, he reads the
Gaceta Ilustrada.
11:32 P.M. He puts down the *Gaceta*. He picks up *Telexpress*,
the afternoon paper.
11:38 P.M. He hears a horsefly buzzing about him, and tries to
chase it away.
11:45 P.M. He asks Beatriz, his beloved wife, to please kill the
horsefly.
11:49 P.M. Beatriz says she can't find any horsefly or even
hear one.
11:55 P.M. A. begins to read sentences that aren't printed in
the newspaper.
11:57 P.M. "The miracle of touching one's knees when one is
at a distance."
11:59 P.M. A wave of the hand to chase away the buzzing, and
a return to the reading of the paper.
12:01 A.M. On turning the page he sees the following news
item:

S.O.S.

A BANDERILLERO PROVES HIS COURAGE BY CUTTING HIS VEINS

FLEES FROM HOSPITAL WHEN HE HEARS WORD POLICE

AND IS LATER ARRESTED BY THE CIB

". . . the banderillero snatched up the beer bottle and
with the jagged edge cut his left wrist . . ."

Although not immediately apparent, today's story is related to the
one reported here yesterday. Yesterday's story was about thieves who

69

accept checks; when an individual who had nothing to do with the assault of a passer-by tried to cash the check that the victim had offered because he didn't have any cash, he was arrested by the Fourth Team of the Criminal Investigation Brigade.

Today's story is different, but related to yesterday's because the same protagonist is involved. In any event his arrest by the Third Team of the CIB of Barcelona resulted from an inane boast in front of lady friends that turned out badly.

We shall withhold names because the individual in question is a young banderillero, twenty-four years old, who on his days off associates with persons from the underworld and apparently participates in some measure in various misdeeds, but this charge has as yet to be proved. Moreover, he still has time to mend his ways, though there is evidence that this will be difficult for him.

It all began in the afternoon in a bar on the Calle des Escudellers, where two couples, two men and two women, were having drinks. They were chatting idly, and the subject of boasting came up. Naturally the banderillero boasted of a supposed feat, and his word may have been doubted by one of the women present, for the men stubbornly kept making wilder and wilder boasts to see which was the most "macho," until the banderillero left the three others open-mouthed with astonishment when he snatched up the beer bottle, broke it on the counter, and with the jagged edge made a deep cut in the veins of his left wrist.

"There!" he said. He had obviously placed his banderillas in just the right spot, and soon thereafter he fainted. His friends, the other man and the two women, took him to the Municipal Emergency Hospital on the Avenida García Morato, where the physician on duty put him on the operating table and termed the wound serious.

Given the nature of the wound, and the fact that the physician thought it might be an attempted suicide or an assault by other parties, he stated that he had to inform the police. Half unconscious, the wounded man heard the word "police," got out of bed, subdued the physician and his assistants, took to his heels, and vanished.

Notified by the Municipal Emergency Hospital the police naturally suspected his involvement in some crime, since he had escaped so soon after losing a great deal of blood.

The doctor on duty gave a description of the man, and it was determined that he lived in a boarding house on Las Ramblas. The inspectors of the Third Team of the CIB thereupon initiated a series of patrols in that district in an effort to apprehend the man.

After escaping from the hospital, the banderillero went directly to his boarding house, where he knew that a fellow boarder would take care of him. The man put a towel around the wound to see if that would stop the hemorrhage, but it did not, so he took the banderillero to a friend of his, a hospital worker, who gave him first aid and indicated that should go to a doctor because the wound was indeed dangerous.

The police located him when he returned to the boarding house with a bandage around his wrist that had not stopped the hemorrhage. Before taking him to the police station, the inspectors had to drive him back to the Municipal Emergency Hospital, where the physician on duty recognized him immediately.

The banderillero, who had tried to demonstrate his courage in the face of an empty beer bottle rather than the horns of a bull, declared to the inspectors of the Third Team of the CIB that he had been in contact with the assailants of the passer-by, who had been forced to give them a check for fifteen thousand pesos when he didn't have enough cash on him. But he stated that he himself had not been present.

Taken before the judge, he was viewed by the victim of the assault, who stated that he had not seen him in the company of the assailants, following which he was released. But late last night it was learned that the valiant banderillero had been arrested again for involvement in a brawl in a bar, though this time he did not cut a vein.—Fernando CASADO

•

I grab the scissors, cut out the story, retreat with renewed fury to the crucial epicenter of my brain, recognize rivers, red trickles like the red blood that runs through my brain, that inundates me, channeled and warm. I then take the spiral incline that leads my body through the abundant stream of my veins and follow another thick trickle of blood, that of an imbecile. the invincible imbecile having now become invisible by the grace and favor of an unfolding of the paper, I recognize her in the sketch that illustrates the page, I could recognize her anywhere even though it's a blurred, rather nondescript photo, I know that she is inside me, I need only to travel along my most vital threads to find her at the turn of an artery, in the hidden bend of the ascending colon. every little internal part of my body duplicates her and conforms to her, each and every I-particle has her name despite the strange contingency that makes her unnamed and unique, at least to me, and that's what matters. what matters is (its matter is) a good many kilos of condensed flesh, the mass that is me, I should guess about sixty-nine kilos, a fair quantity of flesh wrapped by an elastic and porous skin that even so does not escape through the pores, it respects the tangents and does not adopt the arbitrary forms that might well be expected of a more elastic, less circumspect skin.

in other words, here I am: neither short nor tall, neither fat nor thin neither violent nor blind nor stupid nor lazy nor ugly nor handsome but of somewhat unsound mind and not always creative. that is what I am despite having given a different description of myself elsewhere, despite wanting to acquire more consistency and trying to define my limits in time and space. it's not easy to know who one is and if one is, and it's still less easy to complete others by trying to incorporate them within the domestic cosmogony that we bear within us. she is here and here and here (pointing to regions of my body and invisible spaces). she is in the news item in this paper not only because of the name of a street but also because I recognize the work of her hand and her insatiable thirst. if the last drop of the blood of the imbecile has not been drunk I think I can follow her track, insinuate myself by way of the trail that the trickle of blood has left and return to her lair by way of my sense of smell.

I have remained blind in that strange way that means: my eyes no longer serve to help me find her, my eyes do not take me to her door. they now see the life of other people, they have been blinded because of their sheer conformity and are now traveling through streets crowded with people who do not listen, they stop in a plaza hemmed in by six-story houses with a dirty fountain a few palm trees and a little bit of dusty green to give a false impression and that isn't all.

I know that with these eyes of mine, these shitty eyes, I shall not reach her and what does it matter? I have other radars I guide myself by, other sources of light, those that do not irritate the optic nerve. all nerves I'm nerves allnerves I'm going out to follow that clue that will take me to her lair: the trickle of blood.

(and the day I lose the gift of smell I shall resort to touch, to hearing, to taste. I shall lick the walls until I reach her and the day that I lose the power of my five senses I shall invent new ones and the day when the new ones do not suffice, the day that without eyes without a tongue or ears or skin or pituitaries I drag myself—if I drag myself—I stretch myself—if I can stretch myself—the day that I waste away and do not forget, that day too I shall reach her not on account of love or any such nonsense but because I am what I am despite having fallen completely apart.)
there will be a night and that night will be. something terrible will happen on that night simply because it is night, because of its fearful truth. I understand very little about nights and when I meet her—if I meet her—I shall ask her what night is. night is a quick-silvered box, night is another country. I am not seeking

definitions but complete explanations and only she can talk to me without talking and give it to me without even mentioning its name. one only sees the eyes of night fauna, evergreen eyes, a green deep as the sea, a gynecological green. she knows everything and I have no reason to lose her on the other side of a gesture, in some corner where the birds of disaster, toothless and voracious, make their nests.

A painful spot is growing on my left temple, it's the coup de grâce that she gave me one Tuesday at midnight, a delayed-action shot that is now beginning to travel through my head. a sticky pain, the last hope I cling to before letting my inner bloodhounds loose for fear of venturing down secret passages that perhaps don't even lead me to her. but that imbecile who opened his veins to prove his manhood (as if the external flow of blood were something manly) could only have been prompted by her tenacity. I see the work of her hand even though properly speaking she was not the one who broke the bottle to cut his veins. (the executioner's hands do not always make history; the hands that execute are not always the real cause of the evil or of the humiliation, one is not always what one desires to be nor what is most needed. if you doubt it, take me as an example, put me in a book to dry, and display me later in courses on ethics or strange behavior. being a professor, I don't refuse to see myself reduced to the inferior status of evidence, provided it's for didactic purposes.) it was indeed for didactic purposes that I began recounting these facts and I am now prepared to sacrifice my essence, my pale existence, in order to enter creation on all fours with my snout buried up to the joint that connects it to the neck and to the other instances of myself. I have a pain, one of those sharp pains subsided only by a drumming. a subtle rhythmic rattling that can only come from the hidden machine guns always aimed at us. (always? always? isn't there a moment in which they drop their guard? isn't this perhaps the instant in which we turn round and round without knowing where we are, nor where we come from, nor where we're going? many times, of course, I aspire to the absolute freedom of not being in their sights, but most of the time freedom terrifies me and I'm not so sure of myself.)

"my machine guns are all inward and sometimes they shoot," she said or thought or wrote or communicated, and in hours of doubt (which they all are now) I think that the secret of her absolute being, so real despite the fact that circumstances force us to think the contrary, resides in that simple phrase. vain speculations: doubting her absolute reality merely on account of certain discordant details would mean doubting everything that breathes beneath this damned sky. I leave you the list so that you may consider it and think things over carefully, everyone has his own irrational series of unrealities that reconciles him with life—for fleeting moments, for the superimposed time of an encounter.

I, if I can call myself that, if I'm allowed to sketch myself with an immodest word and one stroke of the pen. I (or that continual flow, that arbitrary chain of causes and effects that I call I for the sake of convenience, out of habit, and for an economy of means—three unhappy defects) I have a name of my own (altogether my own, as you will see, is not the right expression, nor the precise dose with which the constant becoming of being favors me). neither my own nor private nor being nor favor, all false concepts, marred by a limping, lopsided, literal interpretation. not private, but certainly deprived: deprived of so many gifts, of wisdom, both superficial and profound, of any real notion of inconsistency, of an empirical mirror to see the inversion of humans, of love in the lost meaning of that word, of simplified peace and the essential sanity I aspire to.

did I say that I went out in search of her? I believe I mentioned the trickle of blood that will lead me to her. I believe I mentioned my primordial blindness, which afflicts me when she isn't around and becomes a vicious circle: when I lose her I recover my everyday sense of sight, I lose true vision and can no longer see her. losing her, in this case, means losing her twice over, it means not being able to recover her until I have recovered her, which is impossible. she permits me to *see*, and to see *her*. I know she's hiding somewhere but she isn't trying too hard to hide: she must laugh a lot when she sees me pass by without noticing her, looking for her when I'm only two steps away from her outstretched hand. she must laugh like crazy when she sees me cross the Plaza Real avoiding drunks because drunks are indeed part of the world in which I find myself, a conventional one and a damp one like everybody's world, the life in barcelona.

sometimes I recover little drops of her, I hear three chords of her rather jarring laughter, or her shadow forces me to turn a corner and it's only that, a shadow, her shadow hanging from another body that perhaps resembles her. I don't even remember how she looked so as to reconstruct her at will, to paint her imaginary portrait, and wrest her from the nothingness where she dwells, to put her in black and white avoiding the disturbing grays.

my wife doesn't want to hear a word about her. she had been dying out little by little as she took on her life, allowing herself to live vicariously. now she is again be, bea, beatriz and assumes her forgotten forms once more and prefers that I not even mention her. with whom then can I sit down and talk of her? to whom can I mention the absolute fact of her absence, how much I miss her?

we're all like that, laconic searchers, and I prefer to concentrate on her, to shake my long mustache and go sniffing about on all fours until I come across the latitude that is her lair. the umbilical zone. her dwelling, rather, her natural habitat on the corner of darkness and unhappiness. there is no longer a way to mention myself, there is nothing left of myself and I go after her and climb steep stairs and walk down long corridors and go around angles and arrive at her door that is no longer her door and I don't find her. I arrive on all fours at the precise spot where her door was and suddenly I must rise to the petty biped condition because I find no door there nor any door knocker in the form of a hand, foreshadowing all those other hands that were there in her place (hands that promise, tense as talons, making obscene gestures, hands for the one who makes them out and her hand awaiting the pittance that I had just given her: my ability to listen).

From the door opposite, which *is* a door, a witch peeks out enveloped in a nauseating aura of fried food. a household harpy with hair like hungry earthworms. and she harangues me:

"The noble institution of marriage, the sacrosanct duty of those who arrive at the altar to unite their lives come what may, will not be stained in this house again, never again will a noble Christian institution see itself threatened by beings from another world. Behind that door you're so eager to get to is a white bedroom, a bride enveloped in tulle who virginally awaits her bridegroom. Are you perhaps him? Are your worn-out knees perhaps in that state from climbing stairs to reach her? You can't defile her even though you want to, in this house not a single drop of blood shall be shed. In this house everything is white everything is pure and the bride will keep on waiting with a smile painted on her lips by a talented artist but nothing else is behind the painted smile, only a great silence and that's what we need in this house: the transparency of day. Do you want to enter? Do you want to see her behind glass? She may strike you as a bit embalmed, a bit hieratic and perhaps cold. We had to do it—condemn her to *rigor mortis* so we could clean her. It sure wasn't easy. Her honey tresses were sticky, her forget-me-not eyes a bit faded. And I said to my faithful husband, my husband in the sight of God and man, who never defiled my body (purity or a lack of manhood—I don't know) anyway I said to my husband: what those forget-me-not eyes need is water, they've never seen tears, never seen pain or resentment, so it's our duty to water the forget-me-nots, to untangle the honey out of her hair, to chase away the bees and turn this sweet honeycomb into something that will purify others with a single lick of the eyes.

Would you like to see her? If you're the long-awaited prince please don't awaken her, we'd like to keep her that way all dressed in white in her white bedroom where everything gleams and it's day. Don't touch her, sir, don't undress her. Respect this humble house where purity flowers very seldom."

the harpy was about to take my hands perhaps to kiss them or to make unworthy and lewd use of them. I couldn't bear the idea, so I ran down the stairs and with my hands hanging as if inert from my arms and it wasn't running away or cowardice because I know that in a white bedroom amid lace that blonde hair and those blue eyes couldn't be her, she the obscure, nocturnal, and warm one. I licked my hand, rubbed it over my face and went on with my search for her.

remember the trickle of blood that will lead me to her.
                                    remembering is
difficult when one is trying to be a gliding feline. to remember one must stick to the human condition that is so useless when one is stretching out through the night and wandering in the forest. something. smell, I need a smell for memory's sake, a drop of blood, will I be a fierce tiger? a vampire? a simple intern on night duty in a hospital with a hypodermic in one hand and a tourniquet in the other? I need group O, Rh-negative, why? because only from the universally negative can I extract a useful bit of information, a trail toward her, yes ma'am. no reason for you to continue putting on this face. take off all my faces, I need a face of virgin wax in which she can model at will the features she prefers, the ones that belong to me.

this seems like a damnation yet it isn't

so I go on seeking her. because I'm not thinking of anything. because I know that the moment has arrived to limit myself to giving without expectation of any reward as the noblest and most deceiving precepts say. I for my part stick deceit you know where, into the most intimate zones of my body not always the softest or the most ductile. I keep mentioning myself this way through mere bad habit, because I have no other way of pointing out to a third party this strange whole that forms what may feasibly be called a person. but in reality I'm only stuffed full of words, words hurt me and prick me from inside what others would define as my belly. I'm looking for her, I'm looking for her in order to deposit words, or rather to exchange my evil words for hers which are good and therefore out of place in her person.

". . . and the banderillero snatched up the beer bottle and with the jagged edge cut his left wrist . . ." the caption affords a glimpse of the very best of emasculating practices. the sketch shows her—not really her but rather a very ordinary-looking woman except that I know it's her—with her hands crossed on her belly that appears big. can I have made her pregnant with words? can I have left her with too heavy a weight to bear all by herself? this is not often the result of my passing through the lives of women, but there are certain women who take me on, certain women who manage to extract some seeds that I myself am unaware of. then comes the hecatomb, the sublime possibility of a son without ears or mouth or nose, with only a shapeless and nameless form that rarely survives contact with the air. but it's my son and I must (must, must) run to recognize him, run and run till I find him, recognize him as I said even though it won't be easy for me. to run as I say and find him and know that it's my son even though he assumes the oddest, most sibylline forms, even though he has no shape and occupies no space.

doubtless I left something in her but surely not on the few occasions when the act of love made us human but at other times, during my nights as a cheap alchemist with a painted mask like a prostitute, able to give of my person only a few drops of saliva or that bit of wisdom that must have adhered to my epidermis on passing through the most abject regions of the earth. (If hashish gatherers run naked through the fields of cannabis and subsequently scrape from their skins the resin that has stuck to it, I too can run naked through anything and add my sweat to whatever juice.) perhaps it was my sweat that left her in that interesting state, she who's so sensitive and I who had never sweat for anybody. perhaps it was my sweat, my tears, in any case the message has reached me and she's pregnant and it's my fault (or rather it's through my doing my grace and favor my generosity and also my madness) and here I am calmly running and running in search of her and coming up against those all too real zones where I know she isn't, where she can't be because she overturns all the reality that surrounds her.

and I felt so learned, believing she could be studied and studying her. ironies such as these at times justify a life and at times destroy it.

and now she'll make the rounds of the bars that have seen her before. the usual cabarets, pushing a carriage with my son in it. will she take him out sometimes, nurse him? is he a creature that can be taken out or nursed? I doubt it seriously, being my progeny and coming out of her as he did one day, if in fact the birth has yet taken place, if it's a birth that *can* take place and not something indescribable floating in space, that tiny bubble of air inside her, that air that in reality is all of her. I know she can be ephemeral, like butterflies, and that's why I can't look for her in the places that she frequents: I don't want to betray her nonexistence and mine, or that of the places she frequents. so I run the other way every time the streets get narrower and start to oppress me in a real and metaphorical sense. they scrape my sides, tear my clothes, destroy what little there is in me that is human and beautiful, and then on all fours again, with my darkest fur and my thin mustache quivering to keep sniffing at the trickle of blood that's no longer that of the simpleton who cut his veins but rather hers, accumulated in the time that she was pregnant and shed in a slow birth in the streets. I hear her cries, the stones have been clawed in a desperate attempt to cling to something, here she had a spasm, convulsions. she turned down this winding street, she stopped under this archway, and despite the darkness managed to project shadows of pain and fear. she drank from this fountain, three steps farther on she vomited what she had drunk. and here I smell the arrival of a man. he takes her by the hand, he takes her home with him.

I'll kill him. I'll kill him.

the long black silky hairs work their way inside my pores again, they sink in, my panther hairs deny me, my mustache denies me because I have allowed myself to be consumed by something that doesn't belong to the world of wild beasts. jealousy. I can't contain it, it's stronger than I am, it gives me karate chops in the temples, in the nape of the neck, a single gesture out of jealousy sends me reeling and I lose my inner equilibrium. I see red. a good color, it should guide me to her.

the other man clasped her arm tightly and took her home with him up those same shaky little stairs. she followed confidently after the man down these narrow unlighted halls. confidently because she's a saint, because she doesn't know that evil or danger exists, because to her we are all as she is, without perverse intentions, without any sort of unconfessable desire. but how about the man? what unconfessable desire can he have to protect her? she has nothing that can be taken away from her, not even what some people call honor.

the man might very well lure my son away, keep the fruit of her womb by me, whatever it might be. I have more than sufficient reason to abandon myself to rage and even violence. I will kill this man when I find him, I will recover what is mine and go off the way I came and nobody will know about me unless I tell it, a thing that I have never done and never shall do even though I'm doing it. a few steps more and I'll know what this accursed house hides and I'll know what the result of my nights with her has been, a result on schedule, more intimately mine than those two beings that go about the world saying they have my blood and bearing the cacophony of my name. our product, our creature, which will have no name or sex or even a line of conduct.

. . .

I knock furiously at the door and no one opens it. the man must have guessed my murderous madness, he's probably escaping through some secret passageway or searching for a weapon or the best place to hide. I'm going to meet him soon, I'm going to beat him to a pulp, strangle him with my own hands. and afterward I'll take her with me slung over a shoulder only this time it will be my own shoulder: a friendly and protective shoulder, very much made to her measure although somewhat torn apart because of all her treasons.

and if there is a solid product of our meeting, if the birth has produced something tangible, that too I'll proudly take away with me and put on a tie to take it out mornings for a walk

I go on knocking vigorously on this side of the door but there's no response from the other side. I try the lock. it gives. I'm tense as I push and suddenly lunge inside a darkened room

I fumble around looking for the light switch to the right, but there is no light. I fish out a box of matches from my pocket, I light one to see, then an explosion. in my head.

there has never been anybody here, this room has been deserted for more than a thousand years and if she passed through here a few days ago then my theory is proven: she is nobody.

a window with bars too close together to get a fist through, a dense layer of dust on the floor that hasn't been walked on, and the constant dripping of a faucet over a cracked washbasin.
and yet I know that she was here, that the birth took place here. there's something that tells me so in the smell of the room, in the slight movement of the air and above all in the shifting of the divan against the wall on the other side of the room.

the match goes out, I light another, and it's as if I see it all for the first time: a kitchen table and as I focus my eyes on the table a glass untouched by the dust and a package of candles. why am I still here? because I light a candle as thick as a church taper and find her right there looking at me, spread out and multiple.

the images of her are cruelly attached to the wall with pins and at times extra pins pierce her heart or the space between her legs and she's laughing at me in the third photo counting from left to right and in the one above, the one in which she's reclining on this same divan when it was new. her mouth is open and she's asking me to stay. I take precautions, however: I push the divan against the door and set its legs straight, I arrange it as best I can and lie to contemplate her at my leisure. I could utter her name if I wanted to but I don't want to and anyway I don't know it and furthermore this air holds it and any displacement of this air produced by the sound of her name would cancel itself out. it would efface the name forever from this room.

my watch says Tuesday the twenty-first two-thirty and I begin Tuesday the twenty-first contemplating her without anyone to stop me not even her. each photo of her offers me a different face and all of them are for me; the fourth up from the bottom smiles at me, the first to the right has her back to me, there's one with eyes that say no.

forgetting prudence I push aside the divan that was blocking the door. I spend long hours in the center of the room observing her photos pinned on one wall, I project them over the other wall with my eyes, I hum in a low, barely audible voice.

where is the door to madness or to some other pathological framework in which I can enclose myself? I'm afraid of falling apart, of not knowing how to diagnose my illness, I'm afraid of exploding and spattering all four walls, afraid that a part of me, only a part, may reach her in her image. I'm afraid of becoming one with her in this room and yet I remain. little by little I melt and I feel that this liquefaction of my person answers imperious needs of the species and I cannot contain it yet at the same time

I would like to put myself back together again, to get out of here and forget her.

can this be what is called love? can I be inventing her for my personal use as often happens in such cases? I should like to meditate on love, utter some clever phrase, but I can't. nothing stable appears to me now, no conviction to prove to myself that I'm on the safe side of things. I should like to let myself go, pervade myself, establish the keys that can be deciphered as their value is dissolving in the air. a nonsensical joke of matter, air, so subtle and unthinkable that it forces us to see the uselessness of our efforts. Here I am, facing a wall with photographs like a sea swell that is shuddering for me, agitating my gaze and turning it into waves.

I stretch out a hand
                an elongated hand
                        a good six feet
                                until it
                                    reaches
                                        her.
I'm always forced to go through these impossible acts in order to reach her: hands six feet long is the least of it, I've had to break other more serious laws, the law of gravity, you've noticed, closed in between four walls that are turning white and spherical: the primordial egg, the alchemical form.

do I want to be an embryo, a baby chick? no, no rebirths. I want a sacred fire to end everything, the photographs to go up in crackling flames. no. not that either. dark salamanders leap out of the flames and put them out and the photographs reassemble themselves and return to their places on the walls.

my watch says Wednesday the twenty-second and I have not seen the light of day. the ugly little window with bars looks out on another wall that is rougher than these four, perhaps with photos of her too, ones that I can't reach on tiptoe or by stretching out my arm. I know that all walls cannot contain her, I know there aren't enough walls in the world for her and wonder if this isn't the long-awaited proof of my love: believing her infinite. but I also know that this belief is false because the notion of infinite which is within the reach of us featherless bipeds—rational and symbol-using animals—is a tiny infinite in relation to the other one, the true one, and only foreshadows a love in its image, petty and limited.

I only know that I'm weeping. here and now. I'm discovering everything that I've been losing little by little in life because of fear, a reversible fear that at times turns into the terror of losing. not now. I now know that it's not a question of desiring or refusing what comes to us, or of deserving what we succeed in doing, but simply of not fighting against it.

I have so many things to cling to in the space of ten minutes: the awareness of no longer depending on my past, absolute oblivion, the canceling out of interferences and vain precepts, and also purity.

from the air of the room—which is her—I receive soothing kisses. I'm floating in the air of the room that is her—she is the air, she is the room—and I hear voices that refuse to address me. I hear voices that reduce me to nobodyness, that leave me by myself so they can talk among themselves and come to a complete understanding, as those who have not yet learned to shape words must understand each other.

I float amid frozen smiles, I pass from one to another with equal persistence, I should like to be at the edge of forgetfulness, to take the plunge and fall into the abyss where she is waiting for me. turned into sharp pointed rocks. she receives me and tears me apart and absorbs me down to the last drop and I finally appreciate what it means to penetrate someone, to become totally one with another being and drown that being in our own juices.

can this be love? the definition of love as being seated on the powder magazine of a warship and others approaching to touch us with the exhilaration of danger but not too much, withdrawing promptly without ever testing our full potential and running to take refuge in other somewhat less demanding and therefore safer arms?

I'm taking on her sentiments, her basic sensations—am I becoming one with her, are she and I a single person?

it's like a dance when I examine her fragmented faces, when I float through the air and confront her images.

I have not allowed myself to touch a single pin, except for the one between her legs in the sixth photo from the left, above the one of her lying down. I held the pin between my fingers, I cleaned it lovingly, I scraped a light coating of rust off it and then raised it slowly to my mouth, taking care not to wound her pride by passing my tongue gently over the point and sucking in a back-and-forth movement accompanied by my left hand, which also made a slow back-and-forth movement at another point very distant from me even though it clings tightly to me. the pin is a form of her, I transmit all my saliva, my essence to the pin. it goes in and out of my mouth and my lips grow taut, my tongue stands up with a bulk as tenuous but as sharply pointed as the pin that I took out of her image and that will return to it as soon as this is over, when I become short of breath and the walls explode, when my ex-abrupto occurs and I can spatter, not without a certain happiness. the pin that I lick, the pin that cannot contain my deepest moans, must return to her impregnated with me.

a long sleep without dreams and I'm able to stagger to my feet and reach the photo—the sixth from the left above the photo of her lying down, and get a better view and a better aim and with infinite precision again place the pin in the same tiny orifice pierced between her legs on another occasion.

put there by whom, by what vile hands that tried to rape her before I arrived? with this pin they surely tried to induce the abortion of my child that she carried inside her. a thousand devils, inhuman demons, monsters in on the secret that contact between two beings engenders, monsters who took advantage of the indirect form in order to deprive her of me, to frighten her away. I don't think I'll let them win this game in which my life and hers are at stake. I'll search for her along the road they took when they dragged her away, she'll reappear for me if I follow the trackless paths they used to carry her off.

to gain more strength and not fall asleep I submerge my head in the washbasin I soak my head and drink and drink and drink and drink until I'm swollen as a toad. and with great effort I drink a little bit more: this water contains a message, it can't be here for no reason, a constant flow where everything else has stopped and nothing will fit because the air, thick and dark, occupies all the space. I want to drink up all the water so as not to hear the hammering inside my head, the drop that keeps falling and which I cannot fight: a drop like an invincible enemy, what a miserable end for this mass of muscles that's me, fearless. but my real enemy is not the drop of water or the person who stuck the pin between her legs. I have an inner enemy I must fight, allowing myself no respite. sometimes he surfaces and throws his sharp darts at me from a distance. today I call those darts hunger. they aren't the most painful ones, the most painful are the ones that bring the memory of her and then blot it out.

Having only one candle left, I sit in the darkness as long as possible and make her out between one dart and another. but it's no use, the darkness blots her out even though she's so dark that the darkness ought to outline her for me.

•   •   •

it's good to be here with one's back to oneself so to speak, and to forget one's desires and allow oneself to be carried along by the current of one's thought without putting up resistance, without erecting a barrier of any sort and allowing the facts— or the lack of facts—to take us to the bottom and make us shudder. shuddering, trembling, that's the good part, shivering and shaking as I'm doing now, looking for my big toe to put up to my mouth as in the good old days, not having access to such gymnastics, unleashing the furies of movement, clearing paths in order to continue the search. I tremble and with each spasm a particle of myself is detached, I'm separating myself from myself, fading away into a death rattle, my teeth chatter out a rhythm that doesn't belong to me but is nonetheless mine because it comes out of me, and I ought to whirl round and round faster and faster until I get the right rhythm, dancing dervishes, until I whirl round and round myself as if following an axis, raising one hand up to the sky and allowing the other to point to the ground as I keep on whirling more and more energetically but don't get dizzy, and thus become part of the universe in which circular movement is the true movement, the only acceptable movement, and I whirl ever more rapidly and large white sleeves grow out of me and a white tunic that spreads around me and now I can hear the most tenuous of flutes, a music so distant that it envelops me, possesses soothes me, and bathes me and I go on whirling, opening beneath my feet a dark tubular well and I begin to sink, I lose myself in the whirling, in the well, I keep on whirling without the white garments now, naked and dark as I am, I keep on whirling, will I find her? yes, but it's only the vision of an instant, it's the will to try to find her, and then I lose everything and I lose the will to, I lose, I lose whirling round and round and perhaps that's what I'm looking for, losing, stripping myself bare and reaching the void that awaits me.

not now. dark now and alone and undressed I'm on the divan and she has gone. hollow, hollow, hollow without her and without my enemies. do I accept the loneliness that I came from or do I take refuge in the adoption of some invisible father?

the invisible fathers parade in a martial manner and we mortals can do nothing to stop them. adopt an invisible father, the placards say, but fewer and fewer have the audacity to follow this advice. adopting an invisible father means running unsuspected risks, becoming unlimited, losing one's footing even inside one's own bed and no longer knowing what it means to feel secure. in our city there are seventeen sons of adopted fathers and one can recognize them clearly—one can recognize them clearly because they wear fear like a daisy in their buttonhole. except that fear does not shed its leaves or a single petal. it keeps on growing and turns from white to the deepest black and changes the wearer into a spider. even so there is nothing to fear from these bristling creatures, they are in fact the fearful ones, they come out of their houses only at night, which is altogether natural, if the word natural is relevant under the circumstances—they drag themselves along the unbroken walls, those that have no doors or windows and only a few chinks to shelter a body when the air becomes unbearable. afterward they move ahead a few steps more, one can see how sickly and sterile they are, and they drag their heavy boots that aren't heavy, what weighs on them is nameless, impossible to forget. they drag their heavy boots and some stay in the cracks in the walls because they find it impossible to take one more step in the night and where they are daylight never reaches them.

what can be happening to the invisible fathers to make them put the few sons who have adopted them to such torture? nothing is known in this regard: the sons of invisible adoptive fathers forever refuse to speak of their pains although by the grimace that escapes between the hands covering their eyes we know that these pains are inhuman. it's this condition of inhumanity that makes them feel proud because it's different, and in our society what is different is noble or mad, demoniacal, divine, or contemptible, and any of these attributes gives them a reason for being, or status.

I can recite from memory, backwards and forwards, the text of the invisible fathers. there must be some reason why I remember it now, and after repeating the text in all its meanings I know that I shall never have the courage to adopt a father. can I be, then, an invisible father for her? am I looking for her only to put her under my wing and take flight? I feel that they are breaking me inside little by little, demolishing my scanty defenses. at times they cut with a sharp scalpel, at times they claw me apart with a hand and tear off pieces of flesh. the only thing to do is writhe in this unknown room with the consolation of knowing that if she is doing it, she is also sharing the pain. each pull hurts her, each cut. the destruction can't help but reach her and we're together as the hours go by and I fight against sleep even though the clawing leaves me little respite and at times I even lose consciousness.

again on the surface of this room, in this common place of memory, I don't know what she expects of me, if she expects anything. her images are displayed on all the walls and look at me with uncertain, different, ductile eyes. ductile eyes are certainly not typical of her, she who has always kept her eyes as they should be: focused on the world. she has kept her eyes untouched by surprise so I could find myself in them, and now I question these eyes and know they can give no answers. only a remorseless humor. and I thought I was magnanimous in wanting to defend her against her own self. poor unhappy soul that I am, as if one could change the trajectory of a comet.

I now think I'm brave to have accepted her. that is something, and that is everything. I'm learning to take her as she is, without an established date or a fixed formula, without placing myself in the middle of the road, blocking her path. I follow her from afar, I am because she is and that's the best thing that could happen to me, the most I can give without even stopping to think about it. it can't be said that I'm waiting for her, not even that cock-and-bull story. I'm always with her even though no one knows it, not even she herself, and in this form of being I assume that she is also in each particle of that feminine element that goes to make up the world. and this is not a dream, no, it is the multiplication that blots out her faces and makes her radiant. radiant, did I say? she must be radiant somewhere, and it's my task to find her that way, as if with a halo. and that's where I am going, where I am going, going

As if restored to life on the third day, he came out knowing. He came out knowing and couldn't write any more, naturally, since true wisdom is incommunicable. Those who were able to see him at the time of his emergence read in his eyes the capture of a universe and also the terror at having captured it.

He then had to change levels in order to continue his search, because in this level she had already been found in a certain form and he could keep her in his mind merely by half-closing his eyelids. A few of us sighed wih relief, but most people noticed nothing different in the city when a door, a room with a rickety divan, some pin-ups on the wall, and a dark window with bars disappeared. AZ's hell left us forever and almost no one realized it. He began to be burdened with too heavy a consciousness after three days of insomnia and fasting. Luckily he had water, otherwise we would have found him dead right there and without a gesture of rebellion. Found dead where? That there was created only for him and then his corpse, after being shut up for three days, would have emerged in the middle of the Ramblas and within reach of everyone. All those who didn't know, who didn't see: the fortunate ones.

But there was no danger of letting him die. A death on paper and in print means a death repeated as many times as readers think necessary, which isn't fair. We could accept the idea of killing him once in order to answer the requirements of the plot, but in no case would we give our assent to the cruelty of repeating the deed, of committing a cyclical murder.

And what if that is what happened, ladies and gentlemen, what if the repetition cancels out the effect of death?

Then he is alive as we wish him to be. We want him alive we want him agile and yet we find him exhausted after sixty-two hours of tension. We keep following him nonetheless: the less he reasons the better he knows where he's going. We follow him without guiding him, knowing that he'll arrive safely at the right port. That's correct, at the port, for his one real *voyage (with boats like quiet animals, the loins of the boats, their taut skin, their mast-mustaches and the smell of pitch). He finds some bales in the shade and stretches out on them to sleep. He returns to his Latin America and for the first time recognizes it.*

III. The Journey

The mere mention of the fact confers existence upon it—not reality, perhaps, but existence certainly. We begin to see him (we saw him, we shall continue to see him) we might see him through the long corkscrew reaching down to nothingness. Above: a Christ of rather false (phallic) majesty, or a Christ the Redeemer, or some omnipotent figure or other with arms outstretched or folded. Below, he has no idea what, nor do we. Very different arms receive him, arms totally other in essence, dark and scrawny. Very old women receive him (receive *me*) and he who is now I begins little by little to take on an identity, to be coupled with me once again, the he-I, I and my other received by scrawny, dark, gnarled, sinewy arms. They take me, take him (take us), more him than me even though we together form a single identity, almost a person. They take him gently, they take me with a certain apprehension and a touch of grief. They carry me away and as they carry me away they carry him away (this is his inevitable fate, my doom), the women with blue-black hair are carrying us along tortuous mountain paths.

What mountains, gentlemen! What forms void of nests, of greenery, and yet soft, spongy, what sublime phalli, what teats of mountains, what erect nipples! The women take us through a narrow pass and with their bare feet compose little prayers of dust. Women who pray with their feet, the world turned upside down, evil no doubt hovers above our heads, and I who am six inches taller than these women feel evil breathing on my breasts and suddenly I hunch over. From my conscience (if such a thing exists, if there can be a focus within) from my conscience, my external innerness, my total nullity and wretchedness, he orders me to hunch over. I obey instantly for we each live in and for the other and I suddenly know that to oppose him means kicking myself in the belly. A goal scored from halfway down the field is a hole that I make in myself through the navel, I take an uppercut aimed at his jaw right in the balls perhaps or in some other equally sensitive area of my body. I know I must respect him, I know I must indulge him, and I loathe him. He orders and I obey, he attacks and I wait for others to defend me from myself, from him, from his coincidence with me.

In short, as I climb the mountains with bowed head, the women guide me and are the same color as the mountains and speak the language of rocks and it seems to me that I understand, they speak a water-tongue but do not lick my face (idiomatic ablution). He (I shall henceforth call him I) knows (I know) that they will do us no harm; I know many more things that it would please me to take into consideration. Or not. That's how I am: at times it transmits (to) me, allowing me to share and share alike for a moment.

Above, perhaps a refuge, where perhaps a hand is performing the probable ritual of caresses. Below—a little farther down, not all the way down, not in hell—us, making our way along goat paths among hills that are completely arid but not at all barren, hills where the imponderable grows so luxuriantly that it becomes an offense. Perhaps up there we shall get to know the place where Quetzalcoatl was born, the plumed serpent, a quetzal bird perhaps and a few invisible nanny goats, a buzzard or two and adobe dwellings, hovels, huts, roofs of broken earth-colored tiles and man's house is the mountain.

I appear to know the path, the gnarled arms guide me along enclosures of piled-up boulders and past dead trees that I greet because I have known them in other times, I have considered them mine. (Something contrives to make its way from I to me regarding the tree: I once knew and would come to know again, in more than one violent encounter, that the tree is my maternal womb, the great welcomer, the master-tree, brother, sublime receiver of gifts and giver of saps and streams of blood that we still can't comprehend but that one day will enter us like thorns, insults or as a kiss enters: painfully, piercingly, fearfully, hotly.)

The women drag me along, push me, guide me, help me along dusty footpaths and I climb carrying me inside myself in some forbidden zone of my being that I can't locate and it doesn't matter. Meanwhile it appears that we have arrived. The gnarled, secret women are no longer pushing me. Now it's as though they were receiving me, giving me the benediction so long awaited (awaited over millions of years, through multiple mutations). The dark women unfold, taking the form of a body and acts, they sit down in a circle, and I am the center of this circle; a canticle oozes from their closed mouths and they seem so motionless, so solid as I watch them running to and fro, fanning the fire over which water is heating in great earthen jars, piling up another more secret fire against this dogs' den—that adobe-brick kiln for monsters, that mortuary chapel of demons.

The temazcal
The hour for his first purification has come and perhaps the women will contrive to make him understand this by speaking nahuatl. Or perhaps they will accomplish this in some more obscure way such as making him drowsy or subjecting him to their will by using some vague form of hypnosis. In any event he submits to them and they disrobe him, without curiosity, without haste. Once he is naked they lead him through the tiny door of the *mortuary chapel of demons* as he has named this rectangular adobe building measuring six feet by four feet with a very low ceiling of matted, sooty straw.

The heat inside is stifling and the smoke makes his eyes smart. Only by lying on the floor does he manage to breathe a bit, with his legs raised against the wooden beams of the ceiling because there isn't room for him to stretch out full length with a flat stone under his head and try to remember that he mustn't ask himself the where much less the why.

A gust of fresh air revives him as someone raises the curtain over the entrance hole, then suffocation again. A dark, desiccated rear end is entering with something like a topknot between the buttocks. That suddenly impresses him. An old woman's backside, a topknot that is a branch because the old woman is wearing leaves over her genitals and her teats are like two more leaves, fallen, sapless, autumnal. The old woman—a tiny, scrawny, squatting creature—puts half a gourd on her head so as not to overheat her brains and proceeds to champ her bit of prayers and to rub him with brandy.

A puff of steam strangles him like a hand squeezing his throat when suddenly the old woman throws a jet of water onto the heated wall. Asphyxia, alcohol fumes, the uncontrollable desire to run out, but no, he must remain here stuck to the soot and subject himself to flagellation with branches of white sapote. The methodical flagellation of all parts of his body and afterward a thorough bath with a quantity of soap and white suds and buckets of water that don't wash the soot off at all, but rather smear it all over. But when he comes out naked from the *temazcal*—while the women outside wrap him in white blankets and lay him in the sun to sweat—he knows of his purification and is now clean to start out on the journey.

What goes down when the road goes up, what is humble enough to take on the steep slope when you don't even know where you've arrived? Look, lady, that hen will fall on our heads, the goat hasn't been tied to the roof of the bus right, that turkey trussed up like a mummy may start flying and get all of us twisted up in its cords. Look, lady, it's dangerous to take so many animals up there, to bring along edible species when up there there's nothing but clouds and a cloud is nothing even though you may think the contrary. Look, lady, you're wrong to bring those little chicks in a box, to say your hen will give you eggs, to hope that things go on normally up there where the eagle's nest rises from among clouds because a cloud is just that, a nest. Lady, I insist, take the goat off the top of the bus, take down the turkey the hen the little chicks, let's have none of this animal life, flesh without words, without a language, flesh to be incorporated into our flesh. The clouds don't want this, if the clouds see you arrive with so much meat they'll let loose and cause our death in a rush of waters. No terracing can stop the landslide of men like cataracts, an erosion of men if the clouds let loose. Clouds are crowds.

He's saying all this with his eyes and doesn't even know where he got so many secrets. Minor problems all of them because the old woman either doesn't hear him or simply pretends not to hear his wise advice in this climb up the mountain in slow tight curves like puffs of smoke without wind. The old woman, he, the animals, and others going up in the rickety bus which is more knowledgeable about precipices than its sweating driver. Down below, the valley grows silvery and the silver grows closer to the clouds that are now tattered and seem palpable.

One goes up astride fear, edging the precipice. Far below, tiny little men hanging from the mountainside plow the rock and will perhaps obtain as fruit rounded pebbles to weigh down their stomachs. This weight, as will be discovered farther along—farther along the way and farther on in time, which is the same thing—checks their flight, their ascent through the air, the one and only genuine, effective levitation provoked by those other fruits that the earth gives out of pure generosity and without the need to caress its flanks with any plow. The earth gives mushrooms for no reason, it gives peyote, and man uses them to abandon the earth and this is what the earth wishes. The stones are ballast, the proof that rising too high is not positive either. We will not speak of hunger because it's useless, not the hunger but the talk of that omnipresence, that enfevered hunger that clouds the eyes. Meanwhile he goes on with his painful, mechanical climb, without even the minor consolation of transforming himself into a nanny goat or a he-goat and dominating the rock, the height, the precipice, death, and even the eagle. Not a he-goat. Not a big black billy goat. Not horns of fire. Not eyes like coals, not skin with spines or a radiant anus either. Not the devil, no, not when a few minutes before or perhaps several centuries ago he was purified with white sapote and the steam that issues from the imprisoned fire.

He can sit down only when he has to, or stand up when he has to get down because the climb demands a bus with less weight. Getting off the bus takes the most courage for forms of vulvas shape in the dark rock and the vagina of the abyss opens and he is tempted to succumb to this vertigo. To jump. He is no longer thinking of her with his gaze fixed on the background of lips that only shape her name.

And the driver recites:
"This bus is continuing on its way those who want to go up can go up and those who don't want to take the responsibility can stay down below because I'm sticking to my post and here we go! None of this stopping at the mountain's illusions or at any rate no more than is necessary. No sooner said than done and *vrum vrum* the motor is running. Get in, get in. Those who have

the strength to go up, let them go up. Those without faith or liable to temptation can stay below: I don't want passengers with a love of the abyss, their passion may drag us all to the bottom. And you, you dirty little Indian, don't laugh in my face or I'll give you a good punch. There's no room for anybody who loves abysses in this climbing machine that I belong to by my own right and because I water it with my sweat and a tear or two when the dust clouds get thick and blind my eyes. Not just the dust blinds me, but also rage and horror at not seeing the curve and missing it. But missing it is impossible, the road is made for me, I know it by heart, and what I don't know or forget, omit, or disregard, this jalopy of mine respects. You can stay here since I've already charged you for the tickets or else you can come along with me to Huatla where the eagles live and a few hawks that I don't name out of discretion and also out of prudence."

The applause was produced by the wind on the mountain; he merely nodded and got in the bus knowing that the sweat-drenched fat driver had told the truth for once in his life and this was the time.

The rickety bus goes along at the pace of a tired man, the pace of an idiot donkey, hugging curves that are sisters of the precipice and the light turns yellowish as the bus climbs upward. How unexpected just when you think you've arrived at blue for everything to turn to ochre, a filter between the eye and the landscape—maybe in order to make the end of the world a smiling experience, or with some other not so benevolent purpose?

He goes up and the mountain does not accompany him. The mountain is left behind, gloomy and intractable. Behind and also ahead, so far ahead that the mountain is on top of him when they arrive in the town after a climb of a thousand hours on four wheels, almost as painful as if he had made it on his knees and much more humiliating. He arrives at the roof of this world of roofs with the houses at his feet and within reach of the slightest kick. There is still the mountain ahead even though the valley at the bottom is slowly being submerged in mist and the clouds converge until they close the entire valley off. As they climb the clouds grow thicker and finally cut this world of Huatla off from the rest of the sordid world, the world that remains at the level of the base passions.

He is the depositary of a name to be pronounced at the precise moment and each man for himself.

The name

is

María Sabina

And what if we give her the name of María Sabina? What if we transplant it, make a graft? It would be easier that way, if we could mention her, locate her within the space of these pages with the transcription of a name, but we cannot. He must go on climbing and he does not allow us to lay a trap for him, he insists:

I have two ways of climbing and both in silence. I have only two alternatives: the mythical and the other. When I fall into the other my feet hurt and I scratch my hands. When I attain the mythical it's the same, plus other internal lacerations little inclined toward forgiveness and addicted to sleep. I sleep, I sleep and sleep, and for what? I am made to wander in the night and I scorn the night, at times I am the night, hence I love the sun and never manage to see it.

The *erection* of a palace set with jewels is only a superposition of flat hallucinations without any depth. The Moebius strip along which I am circulating now is no more than flatness raised to all its mutant splendor, to its madness. Its beauty.

Here I am: traveling the Moebius strip through America because the space where she is to be found is not Euclidian space nor is her time the same time of which we're dimly aware when we see our skin aging.

. . .

Suddenly everything is a maelstrom. I go up, go down, scale mountains, or collapse, and always with the same heavy load on my shoulders which is my own search. It's like a nonexistent knapsack into which I keep putting everything I learn and everything I know or want to know and try to explain to myself. At times the load is heavier than I am, I fall beneath its weight and roll down ravines, and then as I lie flattened against the rocks or with my nose in the mud I smile happily because I didn't fall out of laziness but because of this heavy load that I myself am generating. What I keep adding to the rest in the knapsack surpasses me—my own surpassing of myself, my excess.

On and on and on. If at times I seem to stop, it's only an optical illusion, a distorting illusion because I follow my path continually and with a certain haste even though I don't know what my path is or what purpose it serves. I continue not because they're chasing me but because of my decision to go after her and that doesn't seem possible: a being so ungraspable tracing something as concrete as the path I must travel. (and now I think travel path=wrath. Language likes to play these dirty tricks on us, or rather it makes us see the unconfessable within ourselves more clearly.)

I'm in a state of flotation.

I decided some decades ago—or let's say minutes—to declare myself in a state of flotation the better to capture the currents that may take me toward her, or perhaps toward the other, the María Sabina who will open doors for me.

And at my side, a guide. I say to her: "You touch me with your left hand and I leap backward (we have climbed a hundred meters laughing) "You look me in the eye and suddenly I acquire the gift of tongues and speak to you in Mazatec (we have climbed another 180 meters in deep silence) (we have left behind the mass of houses. Farther up, they said to us. Each time they tell us farther up, as if that were possible. And it is.)

"This is the dust of the dream flower that I put in my pocket as I began the climb."

. . .

Or rather we have climbed and are climbing. At times a smooth path that my feet recognize. At times a rough path, the stones form a cutting edge, inevitably cutting the soles of our feet for lack of shoes for lack of (all that is useless, cast away). At times.

And we continue to go up and this is the dream-flower I cut in an unexpected moment without begging the plant's pardon. This blossom is already dust, I put it between your lips so you will fall asleep and leave me here hanging on the edge of the precipice. And here is silence, ladies and gentlemen, I say without moving my lips lest I ruin it beforehand, here is silence. Here is silence, I finally shout desperately and the echoes answer silence, silence. I remain there with my tongue out and a name suspended from that tongue. Going up isn't everything, of course: to go on climbing = subjecting oneself to edges. With the name hanging from my tongue, which drips little threads of spittle on my breast, I look down because down below it's stimulating: the clouds are piling up in layers of cotton and the little village of Huatla is now covered with mist. Up above, on the other hand, I will find what we already know awaits me and I don't want to meet him/her. I don't want to know her. I don't want to know her and I know her name, damn it. María Sabina. *I am the waterwoman, the windwoman* she sings, she is going to sing to me, as I put one toe in dreams and then immerse myself. In my sleep I shall wander through palaces set with jewels, I shall head for my own funeral.

I know it all, I have foreseen everything, I know what will happen to me when I eat the mushrooms:

the flesh of the gods has the form of an umbrella, these motherfucker gods (they need to be closer to the rains) motherfuckers all of them, boys (they need those tastes of a moistness like fleshy gray vulvas, the vulva of old maría sabina, boys gray and dry and with the taste of moistness) but is maría sabina human? can eyes set far into the skull and half hidden by folds of skin be human? they can and cannot be, like everything that happens in this land at the tip of the earth, in an agony of peaks. the whore. the day that the gods exist, that the gods are something more than simple chemical reactions of the human brain, damn it, when the pain is different and not that fucking tenderness that I now feel for myself carried in a coffin that delineates my form and at the same time molds it. what does my death matter to me, what does my burial matter to me, I have been dead since that cursed day I came into the world I suspect by way of my mother's womb not even the originality of a spontaneous action. and the earth. not so bad, this business of burying oneself deep inside the earth and knowing how it thinks and what it thinks. the nanacatl. the flesh of the gods. the pale, vegetable-like, repugnant, pungent (punchent) flesh of nonexistent, dechlorophyllized, bloodless gods. gods without chlorophyll, where has that ever been seen, discolored, pale, humid, secret gods beneath the rubble, the mushroom the nanacatl I ought to venerate it, and down below:

"We are without land to work, yet there's a monopoly of those who live on what the land produces, as we do, but who've had the good luck to come under the communal farm system and who've managed to acquire huge plots of land without letting us settle on them. As a result we're victimized by owners who rent us the worst land, where we till crops that don't even pay the rent and the owner takes the little we manage to harvest, plunging us deeper and deeper into misery."

Down below is the misery of others, while María Sabina up above wants to force us out of our own inner misery to show us that the outside and the inside are cut from one and the same cloth. The old woman hands me the plateful of odious mushrooms, creatures of dampness, earth. I love them and swallow them two by two, yes, that's the way, with a little honey as the old woman sings and I go deeper and deeper and rock back and forth. I enter the dark cavern hidden behind the thicket of dream-flowers—always that odor, that persistence of an odor that won't leave us alone—the cave with dream-flowers outside grows blacker and blacker with my every step. Ha ha, gentlemen. I can scale the walls I can walk on the ceiling, I can know despite the darkness or perhaps because of it that I'm traversing one and the same surface. I can go on by walking on the ceiling, yes, yes, the earth is so muddy, so slimy that I stick to it like a fly, yes. I do and don't make headway, I transport myself into another dimension and so on for hours though time seems to stand still because in the dark there's no day or night and then suddenly there is, suddenly I have traveled in time and space by simply staying in the innards of the tiny grotto that is me. And out I come again, on the surface of the clouds.

Let's make an iventory: Is the mountain sacred? Does the mountain have the elements of the eternal? And what the hell does that matter? What is eternal when I come across hunger, the great equalizer. I'm not searching for truths, I'm looking for a broad, gentlemen, a certain very real female, a real slut who in a moment of carelessness got out of my hands and became a symbol. A symbol of what, will you please explain? A broad with fleshy hips though I remember the time when I could count her ribs one by one. The sternum, the iliac, the femur, the radius, the ulna, the tarsus, metatarsus, tibia, fibula, carpus, metacarpus, phalanx, second phalanx, third phalanx. And her skull between my hands and then temporals, frontal, occipital, parietals, ethmoid, sphenoids, maxillaries. The skull, *la calaca*, the bald one, death. And the nerves? And when I followed with my finger the path of her optic nerve and arrived at her visions? A strong woman, the kind not sickened by sex, who accepts it however it comes, agonies and all. Accepting sex as it is means becoming part of the cosmos. Asking for love is something else again, it means poking around in the sacred without much success. Does the sacred exist? Can it nestle in her vitals and is that why I'm looking for her? Can it nest in the valley or on high? If it's in her cunt it's in the valley. If it rests on the mountain it's on high.

I search for the sacred down any byway because I know it

doesn't exist. That is, on the one hand nothing exists and on the other hand the sacred doesn't exist because *everything* is sacred. Let's take a careful look: the sacred doesn't exist, but the profane does, profound and prophylactic.

Palaces set with jewels, mines of rock salt. The cold of salt mines transparent as ice, frozen, with stains of color (heat stains) amidst the crystals. And the jaw of a glyptodon like pink coral. And the squeezing together of the times in me, of all my experiences. I still must deny myself love, because few are the elect who can deny themselves what they don't know.

(If he thinks of her he is hard on tenderness; he knows that to accept it is to glide through dim corridors. To search means to reject, only one has to polish rejection over and over so as to wrench from it the splendor that is missing.)

He is now up above and takes on a certain grandeur. It's not altogether his fault: the women adore him, weep for him as if begging for mercy. The women are rocks and rocks weep. He who is allrag, purefeather bird, does not take flight, scorning them because he knows he is there to save them. Save them from a specific threat that not even they can explain as they weep and bathe his feet with tears and he feels an ardor in the soles of his feet, deep burns. He's almost Cuahutémoc but doesn't know it, does he need to know it? When help can be only a presence, explanations are unnecessary and he goes off, frees himself from the weeping women, leaves María Sabina with her mushrooms, and goes on his way.

The northern hemisphere is perhaps not the one that suits him best. He places himself head down and begins to descend toward the negative pole that is his not so much by choice as by birth. When they say north (to say cold) we say south (south and shadow), and suddenly he is terrified by the loneliness of a continent whose internal liquids turn the other way round.

he feels that the search for her may be only an excuse to bring him back to where he belongs. But there is still a long way to go, much to learn. Above all, learning how to recognize the gifts that are offered him, not letting them slip through his fingers by disdaining them a bit on the one hand and squeezing them a little on the other.

Here take the gift of a little book of stories

radiant thickness

bad writing

bad writ

ba

a

of America, and onward

The contact with death begins in Mexico, face to face, mouth to mouth, except that in this case the breathing is unilateral.

And there is the cold

When sinking to the bottom in the search, the cold is not even mentioned. The search is ardent, simply by virtue of the submergence, of so much penetrating into the forbidden zone and staying there where all is blood red, living flesh, dazzling whip-cracking desperation.

He believes he is searching for a woman but if he doesn't recognize the cold—if the cold hasn't touched him—it's because he's searching for something else. A part of himself, truth, knowledge, happiness, the supreme happening, despair? In any event he's certain of one thing—that he mustn't hang back in the search. Once he knows his own inside he'll know the outside and perhaps viceversa. Perhaps viceversa: that's how the struggle is, one day we'll know the struggle but never the result or the end.

He has no reason to let his heart be touched by pity—this is not the time—the emaciated beings that come out to meet him aren't the ones who will distract him from the search. He would be searching for their sake too if only he could grasp a thread of what he glimpses

glimpses?

oh, so little, such faint clarity in this succession of nights ironed somewhat smooth by the sun, indeed easily confused with daytime if it weren't for the beings that inhabit them. People irrevocably condemned to darkness to whom all clarity has been denied. And to compensate, because they intuit something (they know they're prevented from seeing, or from seeing more clearly) they make candles. As simple as that: they make candles and that's maybe the only chance they have to laugh. They also make coffins, the women embroider shrouds as they weep and it's only during the frequent burials, when candles and shrouds come together, that laughter and tears become one and it's as if they were alive.

Some direction for the making of candles (quite properly called sperm candles)

—The wick must form a loop so the candles can be hung from the roof or carried on sticks during processions.

—A white, ductile wax made of the fat of nubile animals must be obtained.

—Soften the wax between the thumb and index finger in the shape of flowers that surround the candle and resemble sea foam.

—Color the wax at times with radiant dyes because nothing must be dull for the fire.

—Finally, hold a night-long wake, if possible when there's a hurricane and the old women sing their litanies that seem to have come down from other centuries.

Some pointers for putting together a good coffin
Use nails made of salt so that the body's integration into earth needn't depend on the putrefaction of wood, which is slow in severe, dry climates. A few drops of water, a little humidity is enough to dissolve the salt nails, and then all is one: the dust and what is made of dust.

Decoration with flowers made of silver paper is suggested for only silver (the color of the moon) shines below ground.

And up above, at the site of death wherever it may be: a white-washed cross and three faded flowers.

The good coffin is just that, a nest that isn't a nest, only an appearance. so the wood must be sought in the heart of the forest with an artisan's love and there must be prayers for three consecutive nights. The coffin should not be resistant to the attacks of time that is already another time for the one who has left the earth's surface and entered its dominion. (I no longer capture the lines of force traversing the earth, I *am* the force.)

(If death is total integration, then naturally life is disintegration and when seeking love, when seeking to become whole, we put one toe in our own death.)

Song of burials
If love is a little like death (a little death) death is pure love, the great cosmic orgasm.

He says all this in the brief moments when he is conscious of the search and then he asks himself if he is looking for her or seeking his own death through love. She who is so alive, protean, protoplasmic, compliant—may she not also be death? Just because she changes, because she can be all women and changes into all men. He too has been all (wo)men to her and now he is only a set of long fingernails to sink into the earth and by digging about discover what it is that separates mortals. Air is like water, it isolates us, and communication becomes almost impossible because sounds do not pass through walls of air and then what? how? when? where? and the other useless questions that concern only the living.

He is now on an island. Not out of love of seclusion but through a simple geographical accident. A tiny island, far in the middle of a lake, that can be reached by boats with sails like wings. He feels as if he were on an island of birds (a mountain-island, again!) and he begins to climb, perhaps with the idea of taking flight from the summit (a flight over water is what he needs in order to see more clearly but naturally he'll never pull it off)

And this time he has difficulty climbing because the temptations to stop along the way are many:

"Come dance with us," the girls with long splendid crestlike braids say to him.

"Come sing with us," men with white sombreros and serapes over their shoulders say to him.

"Laugh with us."

"Drink with us."

"Eat with us."

"Tap dance with us, run after girls with us."

"Let's all run and be caught. Be cornered."

He scales this poorly defined mountain-island, not knowing what sex he is, or at any rate his sex lacks definition so that the people in the fiesta are unable to recognize him. Does he have a mask on? Almost certainly, of course—a painted wooden mask with the face of a lizard. Or he doesn't. Better still a changing mask, that's it, a mask of mirrors so that each one can see himself reflected and, on inviting him to participate they may really be inviting themselves. And he doesn't accept these invitations intended for him only from the outside, by way of what is most alien to his person while he has it on: that mask. Because when he takes it off and confronts the mask, then he's himself: himself there between his hands and himself here, his face.

It is night.

A pitch-dark, moonless night with the splendor of moonlight because of the infinity of candles lighted on the altars of the houses (seen through open doors inside the houses, and the invitation to the dance).

Barefooted and wearing his wide white pants he goes leaping up the street like a dancer, like an athlete.

The transgression of sex is a mask of mirrors. Sin is a transparent, flesh-colored mask.

Living flesh, of course. He knows it in the soles of his feet, that's why he dances. He would stand still if his feet were protected by shoes; but with bare feet, with tired, skinned, bloody, living feet he couldn't help going on with his dance and not standing to one side to let the dance pass him by.

That's why he doesn't stop when they call him in male language, nor does he bother to stop when they call him man in female language. And not because he doesn't know to what language he should reply but because with each leap he is responding to all. He goes capering (with a certain grace, admittedly) up the narrow stone-paved street—the only one on the island. He dances between newly built altars, he passes in front of the white-washed houses, he scorns the groups who dance and sing in off-key choruses, he scorns the guitars, the marimbas, the harps, he continues up the street in exhilaration and is suspected of sweating beneath the mask and his hands move as if not his, tracing signs in the air that the mask illuminates.

The paths that go up are usually the most enlightening, his hands say, *happiness ought not to confuse our desire or our fingers.*

He dances not in the rhythm of the drunken singers but in counterpoint to each of them—he enriches their singing. The drunken singers chant their hymns with more spirit when they see him approaching and once he has left them behind they allow themselves the luxury of inventing new songs.

He pays no attention to changes of tone. In truth he pays little attention to the external or the internal, transmitting his messages with his hands without knowing where they come from. And suddenly a message leaves him halfway down the road where it curves and with no warning the cemetery appears before him in all its splendor. Hanging over the water, hanging beneath the laughter of the drunken singers, the cemetery looks like a black well of silence with yellow spots. Yellow from the flowers carefully arranged in the form of a tower above the tombs, a black well because of the women in black. Here are his guides, the women who have been leading him by the arm on his way, he is there in front of them, a complete stranger to their lamentations. His eyes see them through the mirrors but they don't recognize him. And so he receives his first revelation, perhaps the only one: all that remains of Christ is the falsified message. If God is love then why go on living, love is death. The women down there tell him so as do the drunken singers and he decides how unimportant it is to arrive at the top, to wear a mask, how unimportant love and death are in the face of man's real problems: hunger and ignominy.

He runs downhill, shakes off the mask, departs in a motor launch, and heads toward the jungle where he knows his brothers are.

He knows he has to move on and for the first and last time his lips pronounce her secret name—a whisper. His lips close and he's forgotten it; it's the name that came to the surface only to clear a path for him, and he is received in a peasants' hut, they feed him, guide him by goading him in the forest, they are responsible for his reaching the jungle after a three-day march. Vegetable days, days painted a green that first is prickly as cactus and then turns liquid, a green that becomes mellow as they advance and the leaves grow and finally there is fruit within reach of his hand, and the tender white taste of the snake. Eating snake is a form of initiation, but he doesn't feel it to be so when everything that happens to him, including thorns and the bites of an insect, is an initiation. He goes through the jungle of Chiapas, how come the words of the others in Tucumán reach him here? He experiences what had been her experiences in the life that she took such great care to hide from him, the life when she was aware of things and fought for a specific cause and felt sure of herself. Periods that she wanted to forget because there were hopes and with the death of hope it was no longer worth the trouble to keep a memory. How did the words of Alfredo Navoni reach him, that man who figures in another story, the story that she concealed? In the jungle hidden stories rise to the surface like the steam from beneath decaying leaves, but the decay does not reach them. That happens with her—or with memory or experience of her—in the jungle. She was a queen of sorts and he must know this in some way or other, it can't be that he's wasted so much effort just to be permeated by a feminine soul.

This jungle is in fact *also* the Tucumán jungle, the swamps of Formosa. The vomit of mother nature that can help those in open rebellion but can also swallow them up, transform them into others. With teeth, with claws? No, with no such spectacular means but rather with something internal that makes them conscious of the struggle.

. . .

And again the long succession of nights not because he travels after the sun has set but because the sun never appears beneath the thick canopy of leaves. Nights then with vapors and sometimes cloying perfumes that become fetid on reaching the swampy areas. It is not too difficult—for him—to make himself the accomplice of the miasmas and advance toward them. They have given him precise instructions: to let himself be guided by the most penetrating smells, to follow the course of the steam, to follow the edge of the increasingly pestilent swamp until he comes to their lagoon. They have sought out this evil-smelling barrier in order to protect themselves, but in the lagoon there is no steam, no odor, or anything that might disturb their sense of smell which they need for protection. The central eye of the jungle—the lagoon—is black with an almost oil-like intensity because of the rotting plants, and in the invisible depths of this blackness live all the infrahuman dangers, from the great reptiles to the electric eel. It's merely a question of keeping a certain distance from the lagoon and following the current that will take him to them. (An electric current, of course, not an aquatic one abounding in traps. For the moment the water is his greatest enemy.)

He has learned from the Indians how to build a platform above the trees and sleep out of reach of the dampness and wild animals. He has also learned so many other secrets: what can be safely eaten and what is poisonous: the arms for and against (against others should it prove necessary, but not used at all if possible, and never against those who are his brothers).

When after so much wandering about and so much effort he finally arrives at his goal, he finds them in a circle, weeping. They are weeping because they are attacked rather than attacking and must keep an all-night vigil for the dead guerrilla in the midst of the jungle. That man was a brother and continues to be one, in the center of the wheel of life that has formed around his death.

. . .

A wheel of men and women who suddenly turn their backs on the dead man, holding each other's hands and breathing life toward the others, those others who look at them in amazement wondering how a defeated hero can so inspire them. Defeated? Can these things be liquidated by a mere handful of bullets? No. Putting an end to the essence of a hero requires things the others don't even dream of, and those who know it whisper it to the people who are their audience.

He understands them. He has arrived at the clearing in the jungle and he understands them. He doesn't need to ask the men of the town if the dead man is Lucio Cabanas and if the others are his men who have given themselves over to a useless ritual instead of grabbing their rifles.

He doesn't ask them because he knows well that they are and that they are not. That has been true ever since he met her: every event, every being can suddenly turn itself into its own symbol and lose in action what it gains in permanence.

Afterward they tell him a believable story. "We're on better terms with ourselves now because finally we understand the struggle. We know when we can give battle, or at least represent it. It was different before, though closely related."

"Look, you're tired and I'm going to tell you everything as if it were a story. It will do you good, it will change your ideas, and I'll tell it to you in the simplest way even though you won't believe me.

The long night of the thespians

because in our community things didn't happen in a simple way. Hans played the flute too much and it's common knowledge that the flute awakens the snakes inside us and this boded no good. The snakes were dancing inside our bodies and we danced outside, with our whole bodies, and so the time passed quickly between one dance and the next as we whiled away the long stormy days that forced us to stay inside the house. The house wasn't big, but it was nice. We had carefully laid out the eight sleeping bags in a room that we called the dormitory, and we turned the living room into a ballroom and a place to drink long matés. When Hans was not playing the flute he took me in his arms and rocked me and we were comfortable, exchanging a few words. We reserved words for the performances, not many words, though, because we came closer and closer to miming and the people understood us better that way. As we thought of a play to perform for those of the neighboring village, we started improvising dances as therapy, as practice.

We had two or three ideas, but had them from before our arrival, which went against the rules of the game: we had to give them what came to us right then and there, what they had in essence suggested to us. It involved an identification with the people, but that damned storm gave us few opportunities to identify ourselves. We could see them only when they passed by our windows, and they seldom did. So much wind, so much rain, they couldn't even go out fishing in their boats. Well anyway, waiting awakens inspiration, we told ourselves, and settled down to a long, fruitful wait. Not a bad practice, I recommend it, we were without worries because our money went a long way (things were cheap there) and for once in our lives couples had formed without tension. Until Fatty arrived. We weren't expecting her, let alone by herself, but there she was one afternoon, with her suitcase full of stuff from India. Lengths of cloth, sticks of incense, perfumes, junk like that. I think she intended to sell it, though she said we could use it for a performance or two. That wasn't at all what we had in mind for the people around there, all good people and rugged fishermen who had no time for mysticism. So for three or four nights we used the stuff from India to improvise. We put on the dark-colored clothes, and draped the fabrics from the walls and ceiling like a big tent. Fatty with her necklaces of little bells and a transparent sari seemed to be in a trance. We were all in a peculiar state, and our minds too, what with so much incense, sandalwood, patchouli, flowers of Nepal, and amber. We dressed Fatty in silver shawls, undressed her—at times she was beautiful and at other times she looked like an obscene sausage. Then an idea came to us. It was obvious where it came from, and we should have known that nothing good could come out of so much cloying perfume and so many strange aromas. Anyhow, when we dressed Fatty for the hundredth time and Pedro arrived with the cold cuts. (We ate well and fucked well and I don't know why all this happened. Ever since we'd left our country everything had been so quiet, harmonious even, I don't know where all our foolishness came from.) Anyhow, when Pedro arrived with the cold cuts, Fatty, half dressed in filmy lengths of cloth, naturally tried to make herself a sandwich, and this idea occurred to her as she picked up a slice of pastrami thin as gauze. It occurred to her: gauze pastrami, salami lace, cheese sliced so thin by a machine that it was almost transparent. Fatty put a slice of pastrami over one breast and we thought of the pancakes, delicate as lace fringe, that Yvonne used to make us, and that's how the idea suddenly came to us. Not from anybody, from all of us or rather from Fatty herself. Then there were several nice sunny days that we spent developing the idea and Fatty took advantage of the sun to toast herself to a turn.

One warm night we gave a performance in the main square to which many people came. We even had permission to use the porch of the church to put on *The Wedding* and we were more than happy. Hans was the organist and played the flute. Carlos was the bridegroom because he was so thin, Pedro the priest, and Pancho the best man. Fatty was the bride of course, and we four girls were a little bit of everything by changing hats. First, as cooks we made the pancakes onstage over four burners. We flipped mountains of pancakes as the men announced the wedding, made the preparations, and dressed for their parts. The men erected the altar as they exchanged remarks about the imminent arrival of the bride. They created suspense. She's delicious, I think they said; a morsel fit for a cardinal, a real treat, they repeated, while Pedro the priest spoke of the wedding banquet.

And we four girls, standing in front of the pile of pancakes, dressed not as cooks now but as seamstresses with our mouths full of pins, brought Fatty onstage dressed in her Indian fabric just as she wished. We put a blindfold on her and undressed her down to her bikini so we could cover her body with the lace-pancakes and her face with a veil of salami. We perfumed her with vanilla extract, we put a collar of mazard berries on her, we gave her an artistic bunch of onions to hold, we painted the pancakes covering her breast with jam. Then we let her go into the church that we had erected on the porch of the real church, and we dressed up as bridesmaids with collars of forks. The priest used a big spoon for an aspergillum, and the bride and groom exchanged demitasse spoons. We followed the ritual strictly until the best man said to the audience, "Everybody come eat with us," and we all began to eat Fatty's clothes—in little bites at first, then more and more greedily as the enthusiastic audience joined us onstage and we snorted like hogs, chewing and chewing, and I don't recall when things began to go wrong but suddenly I found something hard between my teeth and I don't know what I could have been thinking of just then but when next we looked for Fatty all that was left of her was bones. And not all of them at that."

"So you ate Fatty up?"

"Well, if you put it that way. I don't suppose so. There would have been blood, innards, things like that. We'll never know what really happened, but something strange took place that night and we never heard of Fatty again. That same night we disappeared, leaving Fatty's belonging there, all her Hindu junk, just in case she decided to come back. I think she played a dirty trick on us, I think she escaped in the uproar and left a few little bones to impress us. Though I don't know. Fatty didn't have much sense of humor, poor thing."

"Let's hope she played a joke on you."

"Why do you say 'let's hope'? I'm explaining a Mystery to you and you come up with the most banal wishes. After all, what does it matter to you, if you weren't with us?"

"I'm with you now and suddenly I feel as if I'd also eaten her. And I don't know if I like her."

. . . a little cannibalism here and there, how nice to allow himself that, how nice to take a bit of things and find out what's inside. Supposing she's edible, I swallowed her up one night when she asked me on a date outside the usual hours and across the fields, so to speak. She was pretty far afield herself and with something untamed about her, or rather trying to untame herself, to shake off the husk of domestication that the others had been watering and fertilizing to make it grow inside her. I went on eating her slice by slice—not the fat girl, but the one I desired—I wanted to see what was inside her but because I incorporated her within myself and couldn't see her any more. She disappeared in me, dissolved in my stomach, became part of my blood. I ate her to know her better and all I got was a taste of her. In short I didn't get to know her, I only enjoyed her for a while and then she became part of me. She now runs through my veins and doesn't belong to me simply because she is inside of me. Now I know it shouldn't be that way: knowledge through destruction isn't knowledge at all. Now I have to suffer the ricochet effect, the knower well known from inside. Her circulating through my entire body and knowing everything (everything? is there ever a whole to be known?), knowing me, and me unable to grasp her, merely feeling her inside me, just a little warm, a little upsetting, because I'd eaten her on a certain nonexistent evening, a night when neither she nor I was there. and I say to the other girl:

"Eating people has one danger: the irrepressible belch. It overtakes you suddenly like a mouthful coming up from the guts, and what can you do? put on an innocent face and swallow again while puffing out your cheeks."

"If only that were all there is to it."

They were traveling from south to north, while he was going from north to south. Their paths wouldn't cross for long, but while they did . . .

"You say there were eight of you before the fat girl arrived, but now there are only five. How come? Did you eat the other three?"

"We didn't eat anybody. The other three dropped out along the way. I'll tell you all about it if you stay with us a while. And if you keep me from sleeping. If I go to sleep I'll dream, and things will get confused."

"I don't know how you'll manage that. It's easy for me not to sleep, because I'm dreaming. But you have no reason to sacrifice yourself in order to enrich my dreams."

This one was young, not like the other one, not at all, in no way. This one had a face and was named Laura and he could repeat the name to himself without modifying the course of things in any way. Laura, he could shout and nothing happened, Laura just raised her head and smiled at him. Laura was the guardian of the campfire at night, and she didn't sleep in order to fulfill her duty, which included telling him everything he wanted or needed to know. Except that knowing in that fashion, from another, is not consistent with his status as a great seeker. He preferred to change the subject, to speak of superficial things:

"And what happened with your Hans?"

"My Hans? Nobody was mine, we all belonged to everybody and especially Hans who made rings. People got engaged with Hans's rings, all those who wore his rings were engaged to each other as a group. And Hans had to go on his way to unite more people."

"Don't tell me fairy tales, I'm a grown man."

"You may be grown, but not much of a man if you don't accept the tales. Didn't you ever live a fairy tale?"

Yes, once, he was about to tell her, and I still am. But no, the guardianofthefire was quite capable of pronouncing the word love and throwing everything away. In short, it was better to keep silent until the right moment. Meanwhile the guardianofthefire made monsters out of the flames and cat's eyes out of the coals, and he chose to take part in the game rather than just to talk about it, to be part of the performance rather than a mere spectator, a mere listener.

Jump, man, jump, they say to him. And he, who is about to leap into the void, discovers that he must stand still so things will happen to him.

"Come on, jump, spit her out," the guardianofthefire shouts to him. "Fly, man, spit her out."

Spit her out, spit her out, the others shout at him, beside themselves with excitement. Knowledge, they shout to him, access through the air, the desire to know. Jump, fly, leap, and he realizes he's *already* flying, and jumping doesn't matter, nor does trying out the wings.

To think that this event was not even inspired by Laura, or was it? She'd been tempting him with a certain key word: wings.

He considered taking off again, they knew that these cloth wings were good only for soaring and that was what they needed, someone to fall gently from the sky during the performance in the convent, someone rather evil, to show to the poor peasants that not everything that comes from on high is a help to them. He could be the one-who-arrived-from-heaven-like-one-burden-more, but suddenly during the rehearsal, without warning, he decided not to leap from the bell tower because he had already taken flight. Laura was on the point of pushing him.

"Don't be chicken—jump!"

He smiles with a certain annoyance because Lauratheguardian doesn't understand at all. Nobody understands, he says to himself as he flies and sees the crevices in distant mountains, the forest, the lagoon.

"Jump, kid, jump, these wings have already been tested in Switzerland, come on, jump, brother, buddy, old pal, comrade, kid!" shout those who are up there with him and have no reason to fling themselves into empty air. They can shout and shriek all they like, he is far away now, flying through other stratospheres that they know nothing of. The performance, in short, can begin without him, a *deus ex machina* who has dismounted from his machine and is a coward. The wings have indeed been well tested in Switzerland: portable gliders. What has not been tested in any part of the world is man's decision to take the great leap.

He is high up and with a look of consternation he sees what is going on below: hunger, pettiness, misery. He sees because finally he has made up his mind not to judge even though he is on high.

Laurala in the distance, down there below in the bell tower, is touching his shoulder, urging him to leap into the convent courtyard below and he decides it's high time to leave these over-theatrical, and rather gloomy and trivial thespians, to leave them hanging on their wings and follow his own path south, toward her. Or at least take the winding detour of hope. As unexpected as it is, hard to follow, and at times disconcerting. Ergo: it's better to take to the road again, seeking himself and at times even loving himself.

Gentlemen: no more stories to listen to, no more acting in other people's stories. One is automatically a part of the aforementioned stories because one already carries enough weight *e per quello non si salta.*

Littlelaura, ciao, I'm going ahead with my beloved search (the only thing I have).

Once upon a time there was an enthusiastic searcher, well equipped for the task. Once upon a time—and what is there now? Now, gentlemen, there is escape by way of humor. And inconstancy. And when it comes to searching (we repeat) inconstancy is the supreme rule.

And they try to get him to spit her out. But he wouldn't dream of throwing her up, or of putting her aside now that he has her inside. Not even of giving birth to her.

Yes, flying. But real flight, the kind that will get him somewhere, the kind that will take him across the entire continent and suddenly set him down all alone, as if by magic, on the spot where perhaps everything once began. In his lovehated city to the south of all souths, the spot that witnessed her birth and hence knows how to deserve her (preserve her).

IV. The Encounter

Flight is of no use for landing in a precise spot, flight takes you off through the air to other worlds where people no longer fight for the earth because bah, the earth is forgotten under the mantle of asphalt, the crust of ignominy. He has finally arrived at his city in the south and it's hard for him to recognize it because he comes from other dimensions. He has gone about looking for the four elements even though there is little water in this recounting of the facts (there is, rather, the scarcity of water, which is also a form of water). Its absence is noted on the heights and if during flight he came across a cloud that discharged its wrath on him we won't hear of it.

He arrived in his city by air and has difficulty recognizing it. The atmosphere is quite different: there's a carnival spirit with something gloomy about it, a carnival in a silence with barriers that keep cars from passing.

"At last we have peaceful barricades," someone says to him with a conspiratorial wink he doesn't understand.

"I miss the sound of sirens," another man adds, as if wanting to make common cause with him.

He doesn't understand. He sees long lines of human beings camping in the streets, long lines of ants that stretch for blocks on end, turn a corner, and disappear in the distance.

He keeps on advancing. They shout you interloper at him insult him try to hit him, but they stay in line of course and so the blows miss him. And he proceeds more and more rapidly, he hears no insults because his ears are no longer accustomed to such sounds.

"Where are you going, you prick, think of others, you lousy son of a bitch, you degenerate, going ahead when you should wait like everybody else. You pile of shit, you bastard. Think you're a crowned head or something? Think you're better than other people? Going ahead like that as if you didn't have to wait like everybody else. It's fucking hard, learning to wait. A lot of good it's done us, with you butting in like this. And you playing innocent. Rat, bum, filthy shit. Why don't you go to hell instead of going where you're going?"

Threatening arms emerge from the long line bordering the street like a serpent, and at times one hurls a rock at him. Now and then he gets a rotten orange in the back, but not often: no matter how rotten it is, food has to be saved. No one knows how long this line will stick it out and the shops will not open until the crowd disperses and the streets are hosed down.

Cleanup teams are being formed for the new day of national recovery, but meanwhile they stand on the sidelines and focus their attention only on the level of shit that might pile up in the city streets, breaking all records.

The country is at a standstill and perhaps it's better that way, a breath of fresh air, except that everyone avoids taking a deep breath because of the bad smell, and as he runs through the streets he must keep his nose covered and forget everything.

Gangster, they yell at him. Fairy, big shot—even though his clothes are in rags and tatters. Hippie, they scream at him in fury, and the police holding back the crowd and forcing them to stay in line and pushing them back against the walls don't see him because cops aren't made to see certain phenomena of searching. He advances down the middle of the empty street and observes the long line of people on the sidewalks and he envies them. Some are sleeping, others have made little camp-fires and are roasting meat, as if all of them were leading their everyday lives. A couple well concealed under a blanket appears to be fornicating. So everything's normal, everything's in the proper rhythm if it weren't for the insults hurled at him as he passes.

Then a family takes pity on him—they see from his manner that he's anxious—and they invite him to share their humble cooking pot and straw pallets. And they tell him:

"We've been here nine days and we've moved ahead seven blocks. It doesn't seem like much, but being closer makes us happy. We'll be with the one we should always have been with, even if only for a few minutes and already it's too late."

"Don't say it's too late, don't say it even if it's true, we'll be happy just the same and our happiness will last us the rest of our lives."

There are eight of them in all. The old woman who spoke these last words, the father, the mother, and five children. The old woman is the one who knows (a mountain of a woman, with a smell of goats right in the middle of the city, and made to order for him). The man tells him how he had to leave his cart some distance away, at the entrance to the city, and he doesn't know if anyone will feed the horses. The old woman says it doesn't matter, horses don't matter when we're journeying toward the sacred. The man laughs a little at what the old woman says but he knows that in the end one has to believe in her: "She has a relic of Ceferino Namuncura, she's a wise woman."

But he says this as if making excuses, and he explains that he had to leave his ranch and the goats in his distant province to travel to the city and wait because that was what the old woman wanted (he wanted that too, and his wife, his children, and even the month-old baby).

"We came because we need to be heard. And people in the city are here because they need to hear, finally, to tie up loose ends. And why are you here?"

"Because I'm searching."

"And what are you searching for?"

"If only I knew. I'm searching for the search, the reason for the search. I'm searching for a woman, I'm searching for myself, for my feminine counterpart. I'm searching for truth, for reality."

And the old woman says:

"You may find all that up ahead, but hurry. You must get there before we do and destroy appearances."

They gave him some hardtack and jerked beef and wished him luck. He ran on ahead, following the path indicated by the line of people. He no longer recognized the old buildings, the public monuments, nor did he look at them for long, because his mind was on his running. Meanwhile the police restrained the most restive, kicked some to stop them from making noise, ordered them to stifle their cries of pain. This is a moment of respect, they said. Keep silent. A solemn hour.

At times the police beat someone to the ground with their nightsticks, but not too often. By and large a well-placed kick did the trick. Police especially trained in Brazil, experts at handling assailants. And with good Argentine boots.

Luckily for our story they didn't bother him. He's on the side of myth toward which all of them are heading: the here-place of veneration, perhaps the motive.

Night falls—his first in a dead city—and he feels that sleep will overtake him. He decides to lie down anywhere, whereupon a man who was about to insult him takes pity on him and offers him a maté.

"What's the matter—are you sick?"

"No, I feel all right. I just don't know where I'm going."

"So that's it. When you know where you're going you can take your time. That has its good side: plenty of time to drink maté. But patience has made more than one person give up."

He sips another maté, two, three, and talks some more with the man, but as soon as he recovers his strength he leaps up and runs off to avoid being infected with patience. Moving ahead again. One must resist the temptation to give up when so close to the goal, and the desire to give up therefore becomes even more pressing. The fear of arriving has so many reasons behind it, the possibility above all of coming to grips with the certainty that one will never arrive: there is always something farther on, one more step to take.

He leaves behind him the man who gave him the maté. Not that he is tempted to sit down and wait with the rest, to accept resignation without prior warning. Running is also a form of action though not praiseworthy. To run after something is to put the machinery of change in motion.

Therefore he runs and feels partly justified. He will not stop to talk with people standing in line. If all he's done is to talk with everyone and listen, that's not exactly doing something for them. To consume stories like swallowing swords is not a heroic deed, it benefits no one. He must move on.

But why is he going on? Perhaps because he heard the word *holy* uttered, and it grew louder and louder as it echoed, passing from mouth to mouth—so different from the insults shouted at him when they spied him in the current of air blowing round a corner. A mantle of mist clings to his body up there on the mountain and doesn't abandon him because he's still made of the stuff that dreams are made of. Even though many people in the line have access to dreams and therefore discover him and threaten to make him go back, perhaps for his own good.

Down the streets lined with closed shops and shuttered houses floats the word *holy* (not the Holy Word) as in an aquarium. He knows it is on account of that that he must continue running toward the same unknown point that the lines of people are approaching. Luckily the cops don't see dreams and if one spots him it's with the other eye, the eye that records and then lets him go ahead, not interfering with his advance which scorns pre-established order.

They have brought hoses out of a good many houses and the water keeps running because no one wants to go inside to turn the faucets off. The houses are deserted now, no one wants to stay under shelter when they must advance like a gigantic caterpillar and reach the longed-for place. So the water runs freely and everyone drinks it though they suspect that the water is no longer filtered: doubtless no one stayed behind to take care of the filters or put in chlorine. It doesn't matter, even impure water purifies and washes and at times they're even considerate enough to cleanse themselves when they move forward in the line and find themselves in front of one of these hoses.

Some try to defecate in the drains that are out of sight, but they are few because there is a danger of losing one's place in line and that is unpardonable. Their place in the line is the only thing left them now, the only thing in these hard times that they can call their own.

He doesn't understand such subtleties, he moves forward in long strides that separate him from the others, make him a stranger. And he feels like a stranger in this city of his turned inside out like a glove. A city turned to the streets as the line heads for who knows what destination.

He feels far removed from the waiting crowd because he for his part is moving toward the encounter. They continue cooking their food on campfires (there would be common soup pots if anyone stopped to think). They move forward slowly, the police at their heels because the police are moving forward too: a sense of responsibility cannot force people to stay where they are.

Some play the guitar, others sing, the rest weep, the air is full of sighs, especially when the time comes to take another step forward.

Miracle, miracle, some shout once in a while and an echo which is people in other places answers: miracle.

Some sell little flags with inscriptions—Holy and Miracle— and a vague image that he can't make out from a distance. Some carry banners, standards, while others give the lines the very religious look of a procession—almost liturgical. And there are priests in the line who don't miss the chance to bestow their benediction upon those around them. But most people make themselves at home in the streets. Women nurse their babies, spank their children about, and all of them methodically go to sleep when night falls and wake up with the first light of day so that the line can keep moving.

No matter how hard he runs he doesn't advance far because the line zigzags through the streets, it doesn't head in a straight

line to its goal. The human file meanders, loops back upon itself in intricate knots, turns back many blocks, chokes the
streets. It is a spiral, a serpent coiling upon itself. He can't
guess where it's going and take a shortcut through abandoned
streets silent as tombs. The streets of a graveyard with dense
trees in whose branches the wind doesn't stir. Who would dare
venture forth in the deserted city (the open, toothless city)?
So he follows the direction of the line at a run, and at times
stops to pant; he leans against a post that feels like a brother, a
post he would love to embrace like a drunk. Alcohol. It's so
long since he's had a sip.

He never thought that on returning to his own people he
would become their enemy but they are not his people: they
are confused, pawed over, and rumpled, and they no longer belong anywhere. He loves them even so, he knows that they're
insulting him for a reason, that they're right to curse the man
who has returned from far away, the man who has been purified.

He would like to talk to them, to reassure them, but he knows
this is not his task. His task is to arrive, wherever it may be. To
arrive and see what there is to see. To arrive, to see, and to
find, if there is anything to find where the ideas of the holy
and of miracle shine. He smells incense and it frightens him, or
rather brings him the awareness of fear that has been growing
within him from the beginning. He is no longer thinking of her
in this final sprint. In the last curve, the last cup (he is completely her). He is no longer thinking of her or of anybody, he
is not even receptive to sounds and doesn't hear when ordered
to halt. He sees no barrier, he doesn't hear the second order to
halt, he doesn't smell the gunpowder or feel the bullet that
grazes his cheek. He doesn't know that he's gone past the limit
and become visible to one and all, just as he never knew that for
a few strange days he had been invisible to some.

He has gone past the last barriers without meaning to and
suddenly a hand grabs him by the arms and pulls him down. His
body hits the ground just as he hears the chatter of a machine

gun. Someone puts a helmet on his head, a rifle in his hand, and he experiences an inexplicable puff of happiness because he feels that he finally belongs.

He does not know if the search is over now or just beginning: the beginning is the struggle.

The barrage becomes heavy again, only a slight breathing spell to reload the rifle and then onward, crawling as best he can through the mud, protecting himself behind the trees in the park. One or two fall, but this is not the time to stop. He must advance by going backward, always facing the enemy who draws closer and closer, almost on top of them. His people are recognized by their helmets, they make strategic signals and he feels good. Accompanied. They don't leave him alone for a moment: when his cartridge belt is empty they hand him another, they have covered his shoulders with leaves and branches, or tucked them into the net over his helmet to camouflage him. They are fighting in a park and he feels that it is good to fight this way, turned into a tree.

He aims carefully and it never occurs to him that he may be killing someone, the fight is not in self-defense, but in defense of something that is beyond him.

"We must do away with lines," someone beside him says.

"We must give their lives back to the people. Their dignity."

"Down with repression and commands!" another shouts, and he hears even if they are only half-words. He understands because it's natural for him to understand, it's natural to fight at this point, so close to the goal.

He feels omnipotent and believes that he is out of range of the shots. The bullets are too concrete to wound him; bullets can only come from him, so he shoots furiously and leaves it to the others to guard the rear. Except that now the enemy is also in front, at his back, on all sides. He moves forward in leaps as he did on the island and takes refuge in the underbrush. And as he reloads and counts the bullets, a woman with face and clothes smeared with mud comes up to him and explains his mission:

"While the others cover us with fire, you and I are going to place the charges."

The mudwoman has spoken to the point; he doesn't need further explanations. He abandons the rifle, takes a pistol, and runs with his head down and his body hunched over. The bullets whistle around him, he hears an order to halt but ignores it. The mudwoman goes ahead, showing him the way. He runs through the enormous park that is a forest, the trees protect him—they were always friends—as the night that has begun to fall also protects them, hugging them to its breast. It's getting dark, and in the diffuse light of sundown it's impossible to make out the two of them, for they are crouching and noiseless. There are shouts all around, at times they fire at the shouts of commands, but not at those of pain or fear.

"We have to get there before the reinforcements," the mudwoman whispers, and he knows that it's imperative to do so. Finally they arrive, they are in front of the fortress, the gigantic box of cement. From a last refuge in the underbrush he looks up and sees a building four stories high, hermetically sealed, no windows, a blind strongbox in which the treasure lies hidden.

The mudwoman gives him the sticks of dynamite along with precise instructions. They must be placed carefully so that the walls explode but not what's inside. The emplacements for the dynamite have already been drilled, so all he has to do is plant the sticks and clear out at a run, returning to where the mudwoman and the others are to watch the explosion after they press the plunger.

He proceeds carefully, the dynamite cartridges under his arm, making sure not to snarl the cables (an umbilical cord that binds him to those in the thicket). More than once he doubts if he can do it though he knows he must. He doesn't ask why or wherefore as he approaches the great block, looking out for his life at every step. He doesn't ask because at heart he knows, and that's enough for him.

Finally he reaches the exact point where the mudwoman told him he would find one of the holes. He looks for it at the base of the building, he slithers about in the darkness and feels for it in the grass, but doesn't find it. What he does encounter is a sentinel who has emerged from the darkness and is aiming his rifle at him. It's hard to say where such a rapid reflex comes from, but the sentinel falls dead and he doesn't know whether he himself has killed him or someone else has fired in his place to save him. In any event he finds the hole and it is the right size for the first bunch of dynamite sticks.

Bit by bit, crawling through the plants that adorn the flanks of the fortress, without difficulty, he reaches the other hole concealed in the wall, on the opposite side of the cube. It's been a long way to come amid the shooting and the bursting grenades in the distance. Something tells him to hurry, and it's just as well because the helicopters with reinforcements are arriving with their powerful searchlights and it may all be over in an instant.

Finally he finds the other hole, puts the dynamite sticks in, and runs away like crazy, following the cable to the thicket, where his companions are.

Luckily they have recognized him and they have covered him with their fire as he ran.

He holds his breath as they suddenly press down on the level of the detonator, and he lets out the air as he hears a great explosion and a hail of gunfire from the distance.

The walls of the fortress burst like a great husk and the gleaming heart of the fruit emerges. And he shouts: "It is she!" and the voices, millions of voices also shout, it is she, it is she, the holy one. The miracle at last. And he sees her once again after such a long time, high on a white dais, resplendent, radiating a silent but intense light from within her glass coffin that is like a diamond.

DALKEY ARCHIVE PRESS

"The program of the Dalkey Archive Press is a form of cultural heroism—to put books of authentic literary value into print and keep them in print."—JAMES LAUGHLIN

Our current and forthcoming authors include:

GILBERT SORRENTINO • DJUNA BARNES • ROBERT COOVER • WILLIAM H. GASS
YVES NAVARRE • COLEMAN DOWELL • HARRY MATHEWS • RENÉ CREVEL
LOUIS ZUKOFSKY • LUISA VALENZUELA • OLIVE MOORE • EDWARD DAHLBERG
JACQUES ROUBAUD • FELIPE ALFAU • RAYMOND QUENEAU • DAVID MARKSON
CLAUDE OLLIER • JOSEPH MCELROY • ALEXANDER THEROUX • MURIEL CERF
JUAN GOYTISOLO • TIMOTHY D'ARCH SMITH • PAUL METCALF • MAURICE ROCHE
CHRISTINE BROOKE-ROSE • MARGUERITE YOUNG • JULIÁN RÍOS • RIKKI DUCORNET
ALAN ANSEN • HUGO CHARTERIS • NICHOLAS MOSLEY • RALPH CUSACK
SEVERO SARDUY • KENNETH TINDALL • MICHEL BUTOR • VIKTOR SHKLOVSKY
THOMAS MCGONIGLE • CLAUDE SIMON • DOUGLAS WOOLF • MARC CHOLODENKO
OSMAN LINS • ESTHER TUSQUETS • MICHAEL STEPHENS • CHANDLER BROSSARD
PAUL WEST • RONALD FIRBANK • EWA KURYLUK • CHANTAL CHAWAF
STANLEY CRAWFORD • CAROLE MASO • FORD MADOX FORD • GERT JONKE
PIERRE ALBERT-BIROT • FLANN O'BRIEN • ALF MACLOCHLAINN • PIOTR SWECZ
LOUIS-FERDINAND CÉLINE • PATRICK GRAINVILLE • W. M. SPACKMAN
JULIETA CAMPOS • GERTRUDE STEIN • ARNO SCHMIDT • JEROME CHARYN
JOHN BARTH • ANNIE ERNAUX • JANICE GALLOWAY • JAMES MERRILL

To receive our current catalog, offering individuals a 10-20% discount on *all* titles, please return this form:

Name _____

Address _____

City _____ State ____ Zip _____

Dalkey Archive Press, Campus Box 4241, Normal, IL 61790-4241

Major new marketing initiatives have been made possible by the Lila Wallace-Reader's Digest Literary Publishers Marketing Development Program, funded through a grant to the Council of Literary Magazines and Presses.